USBORNE SCIENCE & NATURE

ORNITHOLOGY

Felicity Brooks and Bridget Gibbs

Edited by
Corinne Stockley

Designed by
Stephen Wright

Illustrated by
Chris Shields, Maurice Pledger, Kevin Lyles

Consultant:
Peter Holden

With thanks to
Fiona Watt

Additional designs by
John Russell, Sharon Bennett

Contents

Orange chat

Kingfisher

Ruby-throated hummingbird

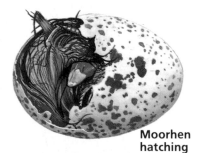

Moorhen hatching

Magnificent hummingbird

First published in 1992 by Usborne Publishing Ltd, 83-85 Saffron Hill, London EC1N 8RT, England.

Copyright © 1992 Usborne Publishing Ltd.

The name Usborne and the device are the Trade Marks of Usborne Publishing Ltd.

Universal Edition

First published in America March 1993

Printed in Spain

About this book

Ornithology is the scientific study of birds. This book explains some of its basic ideas and principles. It looks at the practical skills involved in observing and identifying birds and outlines methods of studying them. There is also information about the biology and behaviour of birds, threats to birdlife and methods of bird conservation.

On pages 42-45, there are ideas for things you can do to help protect birds and provide them with safe nesting and feeding places. Throughout the book there are many other activities that will help you to develop your understanding of birds.

Warnings

Throughout the book there are a number of red rectangles which contain warnings, reminders and pieces of advice. Take notice of these to avoid harming yourself or disturbing birds and their habitats. In addition, always follow this code when you are out watching birds:

● Protect all natural habitats. Do not pick wildflowers or tread on plants.

● Avoid causing damage and guard against the risk of fire.

● Take litter home with you. It can kill or injure birds and other animals.

● Fasten gates behind you and keep to paths, or edges of fields, when you cross farmland.

● Never disturb wild animals. If your presence is causing alarm, move away as quietly as you can.

● Do not disturb other birdwatchers.

● Do not visit nests or pick up young birds unless in immediate danger – then just move them to a safe place and leave them alone.

Using the glossary

The glossary on page 46 is a useful reference point. It brings together and explains many of the ornithological terms used in the book.

Useful addresses

On page 45 there is a list of some of the organizations and societies that you could get in touch with, or join, if you want to get more involved in meeting other birdwatchers and observing, studying and conserving birds and their habitats.

This magnificent frigate bird is performing a courtship display. You can find out more about these displays on pages 28-29.

Starting out

The first step to becoming a successful ornithologist is to learn how to watch birds in the field (in their natural habitat) and to identify what you see. To do this you need to learn how to make notes and sketches so that you can record your observations accurately.

Making records

When you see a bird you do not recognize, it is always better to make notes than to try to identify it on the spot from a field guide. Never try to rely on memory, since it is often only a tiny detail that distinguishes one bird from another. Make notes using the example shown below as a guide. These notes (called field notes) will soon build up into a useful record.

A pond or lake is a good place to make notes.

Always record the date, time, place, type of habitat and the weather.

Date/Time : 6·6·92. 10·30.

Place : Biddenham Lake.

Habitat : open water with shallow edges, surrounded by grassy banks with a few trees.

Weather : hazy sun, light southerly breeze.

Description : duck feeding from surface of water, or just below it by up-ending. 1 of group of 5. 2 different plumages – could be males and females.

Range : about 10m away.

Size : slightly larger than nearby coot, much smaller than a swan.

Plumage : head dark green, body two-tone grey, darker on back, breast chestnut. White ring round neck. Beak yellowy-green. Tail black and white with curly black feathers on top. Legs orange.

Shape : typical duck shape.

Voice : loud quacks, quiet nasal calls.

Conclusion : possibly a male mallard ?

General description: should include behaviour – how the bird moves, feeds, whether on its own or with others, out in the open or hiding in bushes, etc.

Size: compare to a bird you know. Sparrows, starlings, pigeons and crows are most often used for comparison.

Plumage pattern: note colour of bird's feathers, beak and legs. Note striking features such as stripes over the eyes, or bars on the wings (known as field marks).

Shape: note the bird's silhouette or posture, whether upright, hunched, long-necked, slim, plump etc. Add notes on its beak, legs and feet. If it is a similar shape to one you know, make a note of this.

Voice: calls and songs are hard to describe, but try to note whether a call or song is high or low, soft or harsh, varied or a repeated phrase (see pages 24-25).

If the bird is in flight, note if it flies in a straight line or bounces up and down, whether it flaps all the time or in bursts and whether it glides, hovers or soars. Note the shape of its wings and tail.

The parts of a bird

To describe birds accurately, you need to know the names of their parts. You may want to carry copies of a bird outline with you, with each part labelled. Use them to record colours and markings quickly, without having to make a sketch.

Sketching birds

Once you are familiar with the parts of a bird, try to make quick field sketches of birds, adding notes around them. For all sketches, first form the basic shape by drawing two ovals for the head and body. Add the tail, legs, eye and beak. Fill in with as much detail of the wing shape, feathers and other features as you have time for. Sketches do not have to be life-like. They are just a form of shorthand.

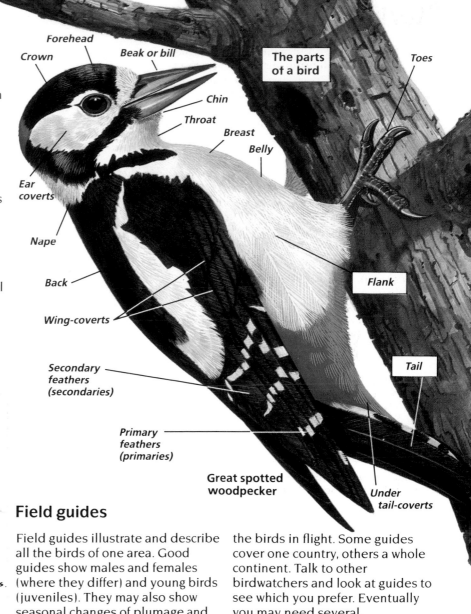

The parts of a bird

Forehead
Crown
Beak or bill
Chin
Throat
Breast
Belly
Toes
Ear coverts
Nape
Back
Flank
Wing-coverts
Secondary feathers (secondaries)
Tail
Primary feathers (primaries)
Under tail-coverts

Great spotted woodpecker

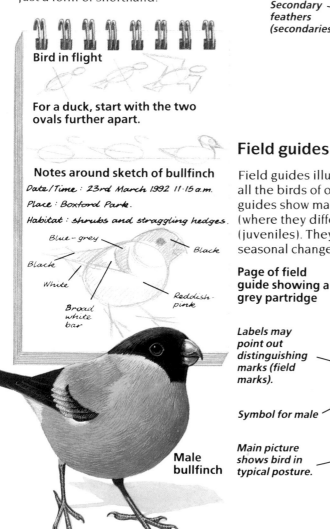

Bird in flight

For a duck, start with the two ovals further apart.

Notes around sketch of bullfinch

Date/Time : 23rd March 1992 11:15 a.m.
Place : Boxford Park.
Habitat : shrubs and straggling hedges.

Blue-grey
Black
Black
White
Reddish-pink
Broad white bar

Male bullfinch

Field guides

Field guides illustrate and describe all the birds of one area. Good guides show males and females (where they differ) and young birds (juveniles). They may also show seasonal changes of plumage and the birds in flight. Some guides cover one country, others a whole continent. Talk to other birdwatchers and look at guides to see which you prefer. Eventually you may need several.

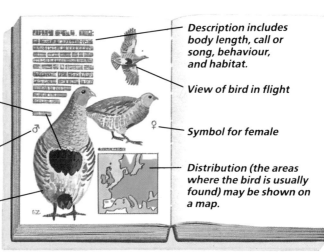

Page of field guide showing a grey partridge

Labels may point out distinguishing marks (field marks).

Symbol for male

Main picture shows bird in typical posture.

Description includes body length, call or song, behaviour, and habitat.

View of bird in flight

Symbol for female

Distribution (the areas where the bird is usually found) may be shown on a map.

Bird groups

Like all living things, birds are divided into groups based on their physical characteristics and their behaviour. This grouping system (called systematic classification) was first worked out by the Swedish naturalist Linnaeus in the eighteenth century. It has been revised several times since then. It is an international system which uses scientific names based on Latin and Greek words so that it can be understood by ornithologists all over the world.

Red-tailed tropicbird

How birds are classified

There are about 9,600 known kinds, or species, of birds. Together they form the class of animals called *Aves*. This class is divided into increasingly smaller groups, based on features that species have in common and that make them different from other species. Firstly, the class is divided into 23 groups, called orders (see next page). Each order is divided into families (144 in total). Families are divided into genera (singular: genus) and then into species.

As well as a scientific name, each species also has a "common" name. The bird whose common name is red-tailed tropicbird is classified like this:

Class:	*Aves*	(Latin for birds)
Order:	*Ciconiiformes*	(From the Latin word for stork. This order contains 29 families).
Family:	*Phaethontidae*	(From Greek mythology. Phaethon was the son of Helios the sun god.)
Genus:	*Phaethon*	(Contains 3 species of tropicbirds – red-billed, yellow-billed and red-tailed.)
Species:	*Rubricauda*	(Latin for red-tailed)

Usually only the genus and species names are used, so the scientific name for a red-tailed tropicbird is *Phaethon rubricauda*. Scientific names are printed in italics.

Using scientific names

Scientific names may at first seem complicated and unnecessary, but their use can avoid confusion. This is because different countries sometimes use the same common name for different species, even though the birds are not related.

In addition, different countries often have different common names for the same species. For example, the common name for *Hirundo rustica* is barn swallow in the USA and swallow in Britain.

**American robin
(*Turdus migratorius*)**

**European robin
(*Erithacus rubecula*)**

**Barn swallow or swallow
(*Hirundo rustica*)**

Family character

In a field guide, birds are grouped in families. The birds in a family are similar in shape and structure. When you are using a guide to identify a bird, first try to determine which family it belongs to. This picture shows three members of the *Trochilidae* family (hummingbirds).

Sword-billed hummingbird

Ruby-throated hummingbird

Magnificent hummingbird

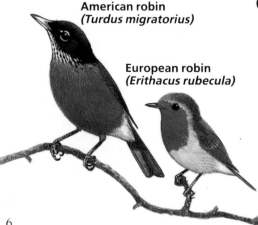

The orders of birds

This page shows one representative from each of the 23 orders of birds. The ostriches (Struthioniformes – bottom left) are thought to be the most primitive. The most highly developed are the perching birds or songbirds (Passeriformes). More than half of all birds belong to this order, which is divided into 46 families. For more about each order, see page 47. The birds shown here are not to scale.

Short-eared owl (Strigiformes)

Turtle dove (Columbiformes)

Sparkling violet-eared hummingbird (Trochiliformes)

Whooping crane (Gruiformes)

King penguin (Ciconiiformes)

Waxwing (Passeriformes)

Swift (Apodiformes)

White-cheeked turaco (Musophagiformes)

Greater roadrunner (Cuculiformes)

Red-bellied trogon (Trogoniformes)

Red and green macaw (Psittaciformes)

Indian hornbill (Bucerotiformes)

Hoopoe (Upupiformes)

Red-throated bee-eater (Coraciiformes)

Sooty-capped puffbird (Galbuliformes)

Painted buttonquail (Turniciformes)

White-backed mousebird (Coliiformes)

Red-and-yellow barbet (Piciformes)

Canada goose (Anseriformes)

Red grouse (Galliformes)

Ostrich (Struthioniformes)

Mallee fowl (Craciformes)

Spotted tinamou (Tinamiformes)

Where to watch birds

Once you have some idea about how to observe birds and the sort of information to note down about them, you will need to practise watching and identifying birds. On these pages there are some ideas for places to go to see a wide variety or particular species of birds.

Starting off

You can begin by looking out of the window. Wherever you are, you will probably not have to wait long to see some birds, and if you put out food, birds will soon learn to look for it. Parks, especially ones with lakes, bird reserves and wildfowl collections (collections of captive ducks, geese and swans) are refuges for wild and captive birds. These are all good places to visit to see a number of species.

Birds learn to ignore the presence of a hide, but you should enter and leave quietly. You may have to wait a while before you see anything of interest.

On many reserves there are permanent hides* from which you can watch birds at close quarters without disturbing them.

Hide

At a reserve, there may be experts available who can show you the best places to watch from and help you to identify birds. Learning from an experienced birdwatcher is a good way to start. Wherever you are birdwatching, start by concentrating on identifying common species. Only when you have learned to recognize these, will you know when you see something unusual.

*US = blinds

Identification by habitat

Although some birds are common and widespread, many species are most often found in a particular habitat. Making a note of where you see a bird can help you to identify it. In Europe, for example, there are many small, brown birds that are easily confused. Habitat is one of the factors that can help you to distinguish between them.

Dunnocks are common visitors to gardens. They are often seen feeding on the ground.

Corn buntings prefer open countryside, such as cornfields and downland.

Spotted flycatchers are birds of open woods, parks and farmland.

Sedge warblers may be seen in reed beds and in thick vegetation.

Meadow pipits prefer grasslands, heaths, marshes and high moorland.

Good habitats for birdwatchers

In general, the more varied a habitat is in terms of the food and shelter it offers, the greater the number of species found there. These are some examples of habitats where you can expect to see a wide range of species. Areas where two or more habitats meet are often very good places for birdwatching.

Forest and woodland

The different layers of vegetation in forests and woods provide nest sites, shelter and food for many birds. Deciduous trees support more species than conifers.

North American deciduous woodland

Blue jay

White-breasted nuthatch

Rufous-sided towhee

Yellow-bellied sapsucker

Lakes, ponds and streams

Lakes and ponds are home to many species of ducks as well as swans, rails, and wading birds such as herons. Birds such as dippers and wagtails can be seen on or near fast-flowing streams.

European lake

Mute swan

Canada goose

Grey heron

Shoveler

Seashores, cliffs and estuaries

Sandy and muddy shores offer a variety of food at low tide, attracting many species. Rocky cliffs provide nest sites for many birds that spend the rest of the year at sea. Estuaries are feeding grounds for many migrant waders.

European sea shore

Guillemot

Herring gull

Sanderling

Never try to climb cliffs or cross mudflats. It can be very dangerous.

Farmland

Some farmland attracts a wide variety of species. However, land that is farmed with methods that involve cutting down trees and hedges and using a lot of chemicals attracts far fewer species.

Australian farmland

Blue-and-white wren

Galah

Eastern rosella

Getting ready

Before you set out on a birdwatching trip, some preparation is necessary. You do not need to buy a lot of expensive equipment, but it is important to wear suitable clothes and you will find it helpful to have a good pair of binoculars.

Clothes

Your birdwatching clothes should be comfortable, waterproof and the right thickness for the type of weather. Their colour is also important. Birds are extremely alert and naturally frightened of people, so they will quickly fly away if they detect you. You should wear dull-coloured clothes for camouflage – choose brown, grey, dull green or whatever will blend in best with your background.

Cameras

To start with, it is better not to take a camera with you. Unless you are already a skilled photographer with equipment that includes a powerful telephoto lens, you will get more out of birdwatching by observing birds through binoculars, note-taking and sketching.

Equipment

Take as little as possible so that you are not weighed down, but remember to include some food and drink, unless you are planning a very short trip. You will need to carry your equipment in something. Large pockets or a waist pouch are easy to get at, or you may prefer to take a small backpack.

A hat breaks up your outline, and will shade and darken your face if it has a peak or brim. It can also be useful for keeping you warm or preventing sunburn.

Choose clothes that do not make a lot of noise as you move. Avoid nylon cagoules, for example.

Make sure you do not have pockets full of coins or keys, or a noisy penknife or key-ring on your belt.

Walking boots or sensible shoes, with thick socks, tend to be more comfortable and warmer than rubber boots, but listen to weather forecasts and make sure your footwear is waterproof if it is likely to be wet.

Take containers for things you collect (see page 18) – empty film containers are ideal.

Binoculars

Pencils

Pocket-sized notebook

Field guide

Plastic bag to sit on

Food and drink

Small backpack

Binoculars

A pair of binoculars allows you see the colours and shapes of birds which otherwise would appear as dots against water or sky. This gives you a better chance of identifying species correctly and lets you

observe bird behaviour in detail. Binoculars are normally described by means of two numbers, 8x40 for example. The first number shows the strength of magnification (x8). The second number is the diameter of the lenses in millimetres. Larger lenses let in more light, making them better for use in poor light, but add to the weight of the binoculars.

Puffins viewed without binoculars

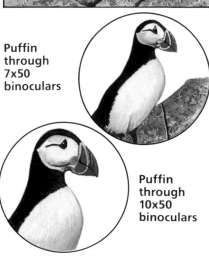

Puffin through 7x50 binoculars

Puffin through 10x50 binoculars

Never look at the sun or bright lights through binoculars.

Buying binoculars

A good first pair of binoculars for general use is either 8x30 or 8x40. Avoid 10x50 to start with as they are heavy and hard to hold steady. Always try binoculars outdoors before you buy them and check the points listed on the right.

When you have bought your binoculars, practise focusing at various distances. This will help you to find birds quickly when birdwatching. Also, shorten the strap so the binoculars hang comfortably on your chest.

- Are the binoculars a comfortable size for your hands?
- Do they feel too heavy to hold up to your eyes for long?
- Do the eyecups (see below) keep out stray side-light?
- Does the focusing knob turn smoothly with your finger tips?
- Is the image sharp without any sign of a rainbow halo around it?
- Do vertical objects (e.g. telephone poles) look straight?

Adjusting binoculars

Your binoculars must be adjusted to your eyes before you can use them. To focus your left eye, cover the right objective lens with the lens cap or your hand and turn the focusing knob until your left eye has a clear image. To focus your right eye, cover the left objective lens and then use the adjusting eyepiece. Once you have adjusted your binoculars in this way, you do not need to use the adjusting eyepiece again. Keep it in the same position and use the focusing knob when necessary.

Adjusting eyepiece

Eyecups

Focusing knob

Objective lens

Telescopes

Telescopes can be used to study birds on the ground or in water. The high magnification gives excellent views, but telescopes can be expensive and heavy to carry. They also need to be supported, usually on a tripod. Magnification is most often x20, but a zoom lens gives magnification up to x60 in good light.

Telescopes are especially useful for watching birds on beaches and out at sea.

Tripod

Developing your skills

It takes skill, understanding and patience to get close to birds in the field without being detected. The techniques that you will need to develop in order to do this are known as fieldcraft.

To get the most out of ornithology, you also need to be aware of the best times to observe birds, since in most areas of the world, the amount of bird activity varies according to the time of day or the time of year.

Northern cardinals are residents of North America.

Seasonal changes

In most parts of the world, the amount of birdlife and the variety of species change from season to season. Birds stay in one area to breed and raise young. At other times they may move around to find food, or even migrate away completely (see pages 34-35). Field guides tell you how likely you are to see a bird and at which time of year by describing birds as residents, migrants or vagrants.

Pied flycatchers are summer visitors to Europe and spend the European winter in Africa.

- A resident is a bird that stays in one area all year round, for example a northern cardinal.

- A migrant is a bird that divides its time between two areas, according to the seasons, for example a pied flycatcher.

Arctic terns are seen along coasts of Europe and North America during their migrations. They nest in the Arctic and spend the winter near the Antarctic.

- A bird is described as a passage migrant when it passes through an area during its migration.

Yellow-billed cuckoos are occasionally seen in Europe as rare vagrants from North America.

- A bird is described as a vagrant when it is seen far outside its normal range because it has been blown off course or has become lost while migrating.

Timing the tides

To see waders and other shore birds, it is best to visit tidal areas just before or just after high tide. At high tide, many fly off to roost above the high water mark. By low tide, the areas of sand or mud may be so big that birds will be distant specks, even with the aid of binoculars.

Waders feeding on a mudflat

The early bird

You need to get up early to study birds, as most birds are at their most active early in the morning. At this time, they search busily for food to restore energy levels depleted by the effort of keeping warm during the night.

During the breeding season, birds are especially active and many can be seen throughout the day as they fly to and from their nests with food for their young. The dawn chorus is also extra noisy at this time of year.

In Europe, blackbirds are early contributors to the dawn chorus.

Fieldcraft

There are two ways of getting close enough to observe wild birds. You can either stalk them, like a hunter stalking prey, or you can choose a suitable spot and wait to see birds that come to you. The "wait and see" method is best to try first. It can be done in the open as well as in a hide. Choose a place where you are likely to see birds and make yourself as comfortable as possible. Keep behind cover, or disguise your shape by sitting in front of a bush, boulder or tree. Sit with the sun behind you so you do not have to squint and so light does not reflect off your binoculars. Keep very quiet and still.

Red-capped tobin

Crimson rosella

Brolga cranes

If you listen carefully, you may recognize some of the birds' calls (see pages 24-25).

Learning to stalk

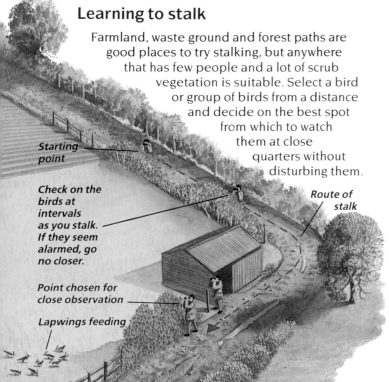

Farmland, waste ground and forest paths are good places to try stalking, but anywhere that has few people and a lot of scrub vegetation is suitable. Select a bird or group of birds from a distance and decide on the best spot from which to watch them at close quarters without disturbing them.

Starting point

Check on the birds at intervals as you stalk. If they seem alarmed, go no closer.

Route of stalk

Point chosen for close observation

Lapwings feeding

Cover

When stalking, you must consider cover first. You do not need to be totally hidden all the time but you must disguise your shape. Try not to stand against the skyline in open habitats. Work out the route which offers the most cover before you start.

Care

Take care how you move. Walk slowly and quietly. Avoid puddles and dry vegetation. Be especially careful with woodpigeons and jays, which make a lot of noise if they detect you, and alert other birds. Do not disturb feeding birds in winter.

Concentration

Concentration is essential. As well as keeping a constant eye on the birds, you must be alert to everything around you, so you can adjust your movements or route if necessary. One lapse in concentration can ruin a carefully planned stalk.

Feathers and flying

As well as enabling them to fly, feathers keep birds warm and give them shape, colour and a windproof and waterproof covering. For some birds, feathers are important for camouflage and in courtship displays (see pages 28-29). Although feathers make up only about a sixth of a bird's weight, even small birds have about 1000. Some swans have more than 25,000.

Types of feathers

The feathers you see when you look at a bird are the flight feathers of the wings and tail and the contour feathers that cover the body. Underneath the contour feathers are soft down feathers and hair-like feathers called filoplumes, which are thought to keep contour feathers in place.

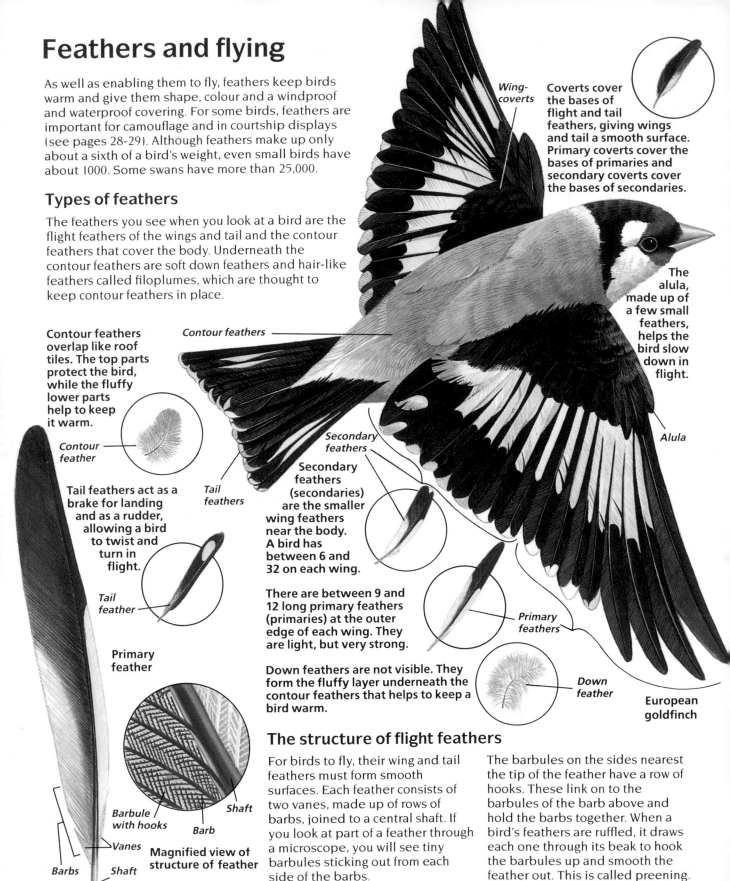

Wing-coverts

Coverts cover the bases of flight and tail feathers, giving wings and tail a smooth surface. Primary coverts cover the bases of primaries and secondary coverts cover the bases of secondaries.

The alula, made up of a few small feathers, helps the bird slow down in flight.

Alula

Contour feathers overlap like roof tiles. The top parts protect the bird, while the fluffy lower parts help to keep it warm.

Contour feathers

Contour feather

Tail feathers act as a brake for landing and as a rudder, allowing a bird to twist and turn in flight.

Tail feathers

Tail feather

Primary feather

Secondary feathers

Secondary feathers (secondaries) are the smaller wing feathers near the body. A bird has between 6 and 32 on each wing.

There are between 9 and 12 long primary feathers (primaries) at the outer edge of each wing. They are light, but very strong.

Down feathers are not visible. They form the fluffy layer underneath the contour feathers that helps to keep a bird warm.

Primary feathers

Down feather

European goldfinch

Barbule with hooks

Shaft

Barb

Vanes

Magnified view of structure of feather

Barbs

Shaft

The structure of flight feathers

For birds to fly, their wing and tail feathers must form smooth surfaces. Each feather consists of two vanes, made up of rows of barbs, joined to a central shaft. If you look at part of a feather through a microscope, you will see tiny barbules sticking out from each side of the barbs.

The barbules on the sides nearest the tip of the feather have a row of hooks. These link on to the barbules of the barb above and hold the barbs together. When a bird's feathers are ruffled, it draws each one through its beak to hook the barbules up and smooth the feather out. This is called preening.

Flying

Most birds' bodies are well adapted for flying. Their skeletons are extremely light because most of their bones are hollow. Their wings are powered by large muscles on either side of the breastbone. These muscles are attached to a large extension of the breastbone, called the keel.

Tawny owl

Large muscles power wings

Keel

Wings have a curved shape which helps birds to fly. Moving air flows faster over the curve than under it. As a result, air pressure is greatest under the wings and this lifts the bird up.

Air flows faster over wings than under them.

Herring gull

To slow down, a bird alters the angle of its wings. It also raises its alulas which helps keep the air flowing smoothly over the wings. In most birds, the primaries are opened up to allow air through and reduce air resistance. All this allows a bird to slow down and land in a controlled fashion.

Herring gull about to land

Alula

Primaries opened

Feet lowered

Tail held down and spread out acts as brake.

Types of flight

Birds fly by flapping, gliding or soaring on air currents, and some species can hover. In flapping flight, a bird moves its wings forward and down on the downstroke with the primaries held flat to push against the air and pull the bird forward. On the upstroke, it brings its wings up and back with the primaries separated to let air through.

Goldcrest flapping

Primaries separated

Primaries held flat

Kittiwake gliding

In gliding flight, birds hold out their wings stiffly to catch air currents. In soaring, they use up-currents to gain height. Only hummingbirds are capable of continuous hovering flight. Their wings move in a very fast, non-stop figure-of-eight.

Hummingbird hovering

Wing shapes

Wing shapes reflect their uses. Fast flight generally requires narrow wings, whereas slow flight needs a larger surface area. There are four main shapes for different types of flight.

Sparrowhawks, jays and many perching birds have short, broad, rounded wings for weaving among trees.

Swifts, swallows and falcons have pointed wings, tending to be swept backward, for high-speed flying.

Long-distance gliders, such as shearwaters and albatrosses, have long, narrow, pointed wings.

Eagles, vultures and storks have large, wide wings with emarginated outer primaries (see right). These wings are for gliding at low speeds and soaring.

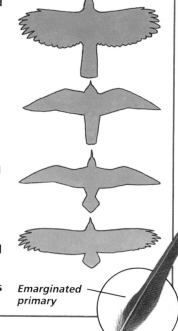

Emarginated primary

Feather colour and care

A bird's feathers all together are called its plumage. Birds have an amazing variety of different plumage colours and patterns. Colour is not always a reliable means of identification, however, as many species' plumage changes according to the time of year, the age and sex of the birds and even the food they eat.

Plumage patterns

Plumage colour and pattern play an important part in the lives of birds. Females often have dull plumage and markings that match their backgrounds so that they are not easily seen while they are nesting. Many males have brightly-coloured or showy plumage to help them attract mates.

A male black grouse has showy plumage to impress females. A female has dull-coloured plumage.

A number of species, such as plovers, have plumage which makes them difficult to see because it breaks up their outline. Other birds have striking markings such as wing bars or a white rump. These help make sure that they do not lose sight of one another when they are flying in a flock.

Semipalmated plovers have markings which break up their outlines, so they are hard to see against their background.

Greylag geese follow each other's white rumps in flight.

Feather care

As birds go about their everyday activities, their feathers become dirty and untidy. Frequent preening (see page 14) helps to keep their feathers in good condition. Bathing also helps to clean feathers and remove parasites, such as lice, mites and fleas, which suck blood or eat feathers.

When preening, a bird spreads oil on to its feathers from the preen gland on its rump. This helps to waterproof them.

Greater flamingo

As it preens, a flamingo exposes the brightly coloured wing feathers that are normally hidden, except when it is flying. A flamingo's colour comes from the food it eats – shrimps and other small water animals. If a flamingo is fed the wrong diet, it begins to lose its colour.

Moulting

Feathers do eventually become worn, especially during the breeding season when birds are very active. They are shed and replaced in the process of moulting. Most birds moult once a year, after breeding. New feathers develop in protective sheaths in tiny pits in the skin. They push out the old ones as they grow.

A feather developing

Protective sheath

Flight feathers are shed and replaced in an order that usually allows a bird to continue flying while moulting takes place. Some species such as ducks, however, lose all their primaries and secondaries at once and cannot fly for several weeks. During this time, male ducks moult into a less colourful plumage, called eclipse plumage, which makes them less conspicuous while they cannot fly.

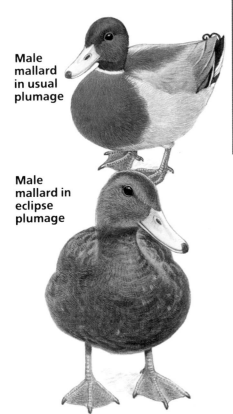

Male mallard in usual plumage

Male mallard in eclipse plumage

Seasonal colour changes

Some species look different in summer and winter because they moult twice a year – in spring, and again after breeding. Others, which moult once a year, may have light-coloured tips to their feathers that wear away before breeding to reveal a brighter plumage.

Dunlin have different summer and winter plumages as a result of moulting twice a year.

Winter

Summer

Starlings are more colourful in spring and summer when many of their light feather tips have worn away.

Spring

Autumn

Plumage development

Young birds have a covering of downy feathers to keep them warm. As they grow, they develop their first set of feathers for flying, called juvenile plumage. They are often a different colour from the adult's. Juvenile plumage is moulted in the autumn, usually giving way to adult plumage, though some larger birds take two or more years to reach the adult state. Herring gulls take four years to develop full adult plumage. Each of the immature, or sub-adult, plumages is slightly different.

Herring gull plumages

1 Juvenile plumage

2 Immature or sub-adult plumage, first winter

3 Immature plumage, second winter

5 Adult summer breeding plumage, fourth year

4 Immature plumage, third winter

Collecting wing feathers

Choose an open space, such as an area of wasteground or sports field, where you regularly see a flock of birds, such as pigeons or gulls. Visit it every day after the breeding season, and search for wing feathers. Label each one with the date on which you found it. If you find enough, you may be able to decide on the position of each feather in a wing and find out the order in which they were moulted.

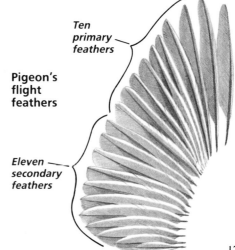

Ten primary feathers

Pigeon's flight feathers

Eleven secondary feathers

Bird detection

We see birds every day, but their lives may be very secretive. Many species do, however, leave some clues behind, especially remains of meals. With careful detective work, these can help provide information about behaviour and feeding habits.

Pellets

Many birds swallow their food whole. The parts they cannot digest, such as bones, fur, feathers and hard parts of insects are later regurgitated (coughed up) in the form of compact parcels called pellets.

Over 330 species produce pellets, including garden birds such as starlings. Look out for different pellets at feeding, roosting and nesting places.

Barn owl pellet

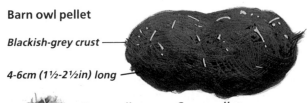

Blackish-grey crust

4-6cm (1½-2½in) long

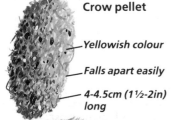

Crow pellet

Yellowish colour

Falls apart easily

4-4.5cm (1½-2in) long

Crow pellets may contain parts of insects, small stones and plant stems. A crow that has been eating small mammals produces a darker, firmer pellet with bones in it. Crow pellets are found near nest sites and in fields.

Darker, firmer crow pellet

Kestrel pellet

Mammal fur

3-5.5cm (1-2in) long

The pellets of birds of prey are found under perches, such as power lines, and in old buildings. These birds tear flesh and fur from their prey, so any bones in their pellets are often broken.

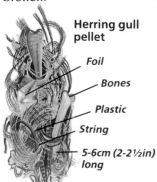

Herring gull pellet

Foil

Bones

Plastic

String

5-6cm (2-2½in) long

Gulls have a very varied diet. Those that forage on rubbish dumps eat all sorts of things. Pieces of plastic and metal, large bones and even lumps of glass may be found in their pellets.

Examining owl pellets

By examining the contents of a pellet, you can get an idea of what a bird has been eating. Owl pellets are best for examination. Since an owl's digestive system is very poor at digesting bones, their pellets may contain all the parts of a skeleton.

To examine a pellet you will need a small bowl of warm water, two cocktail sticks (or large needles), some newspaper, a pair of tweezers, a soft paint brush and some paper towels. A magnifying glass is also useful.

Do not touch any part of the pellet with your hands.

1. Soak the pellet in water for an hour. Put it on newspaper, then gently prise it apart with the sticks or needles.

2. Using the tweezers, carefully remove hard parts and bones and pull off any fur that is sticking to them.

3. Clean each part with the paint brush. Wash them and dry them with kitchen paper.

4. Try to identify any skulls (a magnifying glass is helpful). Use an identification leaflet (from some bird societies – see page 45) or a good reference book to help you.

As well as bones of small mammals such as voles, shrews and mice, you may find bones and beaks of birds, and insect wing cases. Keep your finds in boxes or stick them onto cardboard with clear glue and label them.*

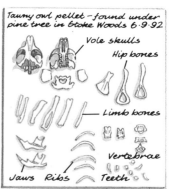

Tawny owl pellet – found under pine tree in Stoke Woods 6.9.92

Vole skulls

Hip bones

Limb bones

Vertebrae

Jaws Ribs Teeth

*Always wash your hands after examining pellets.

Feathers

Discarded feathers are an obvious clue to the presence of birds. As most birds moult every year (see page 17), there are a wide variety to be found. Moulted feathers often show signs of wear at the tips, but the shaft is usually undamaged.

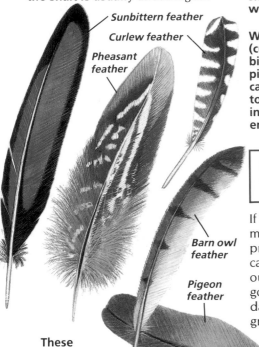

- **Sunbittern feather**
- **Curlew feather**
- **Pheasant feather**
- **Barn owl feather**
- **Pigeon feather**

These feathers are not to scale.

You can tape any feathers that you find into a note book with a note next to each one to show where it was found.

Curlew flight feather found July 3 '92 at Betterton Bay.

Whole wings (cut from dead birds) can be pinned to cardboard, left to dry and kept in a large envelope.

Remember to wash your hands every time you handle feathers.

If there is flesh on a feather, it means that it was pulled out, probably because the bird was caught by a predator. A feather torn out by a bird of prey, such as a goshawk or falcon, often has a damaged shaft where it was grasped in the bird's beak.

- **Damaged shaft**

Goshawk on plucking post

Woodpigeon feathers

A lot of feathers in one place show that a bird has been killed. This is evident near a "plucking post" – a feeding place such as a rock, used regularly by a bird of prey.

Feeding signs

Many species of birds have specialized ways of feeding that leave behind recognizable traces. Song thrushes, for example, often feed on snails, smashing the shells on a hard object, such as a stone or tree stump. The same object may be used many times and is known as a thrush's anvil.

Song thrush on thrush's anvil

Nuthatches and woodpeckers wedge nuts in crevices to hold them steady. Shells and half-eaten nuts may be found in crevices.

Hazel nuts wedged in tree bark by a nuthatch

Cones which have been attacked by crossbills have a distinctive appearance. The birds use their bills (see page 23) to split and twist the scales of the cones to reach the seeds to eat.

Pine cone attacked by a crossbill

Some species of shrike store food in "larders", impaling their prey on barbed wire or on thorns to be eaten later. Shrikes are often called "butcher birds" from this habit.

Lizard impaled on thorns by a loggerhead shrike

Loggerhead shrike

Feet and tracks

Most birds mainly use their wings, rather than their legs and feet, for getting around, but feet are used for a wide range of other activities such as swimming, perching, climbing, wading, digging, holding food and catching and killing prey.

Ostrich foot

The majority of species have four toes on each foot, though some have three. The ostrich is the only bird that has just two. The most common arrangement of toes is three facing forward and one backward, though parrots and woodpeckers have two facing forward and two facing backward to help them climb trees.

Most birds have 4 toes.

Perching birds

A perching bird's toes automatically clamp on to branches with a grip so firm that a bird can sleep without falling off. The arrangement of its toes also allows it to move freely on the ground. Its leg muscles, ankles and knees are close to the body to give better balance in flight. Below the ankles, birds have only bones, tendons and blood vessels, so their legs are very thin.

Blue jay

Knee hidden by feathers

Ankle

Adaptation

Birds' feet and legs are adapted for their different habitats and lifestyles. For example, many wading birds, which spend most of their time in or by water, have long legs which allow them to search for food in deep water. Their feet have lost much of their power to grip and in many species the hind toe has become very small and may not touch the ground. In some it has disappeared completely. Birds such as swifts, which spend most of their lives on the wing, have little use for feet and legs except when they are nesting. Their legs have become so short and weak that they cannot walk on the ground or perch on branches or posts.

The osprey, a large bird of prey, uses its huge claws to snatch up fish as it swoops down on to the water.

Outer forward toe turned backward to give better hold on prey

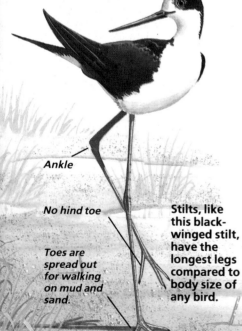

Ankle

No hind toe

Toes are spread out for walking on mud and sand.

Stilts, like this black-winged stilt, have the longest legs compared to body size of any bird.

Swifts can cling to buildings and rocks, before they enter their nests, but they are unable to walk on the ground or perch on branches.

Swifts have 4 tiny toes with sharp claws.

Finding tracks

Many birds' tracks are hard to find because the birds have small feet, are light, and spend little time on the ground. Look for tracks in snow, mud or sand, on mudflats, seashores and riverbanks and around ponds, lakes or puddles. Note the size and shape of any you find and whether alternate or paired. Birds that walk or run make alternate tracks. They may leave an almost straight line, or a zig-zag pattern. Paired tracks are made by birds that hop.

Pheasant

Straight alternate tracks

Pigeon

Zig-zag alternate tracks

Blackbird

Paired tracks

Water birds' tracks

The tracks of water birds are among those that you are most likely to see. In birds that swim often, the foot has become a paddle with webbing, which makes the tracks easier to recognize.

Anhingas and others in their family have all 4 toes joined by webbing. Rails, such as moorhens, have long, widely spread toes, for walking on mud or water plants.

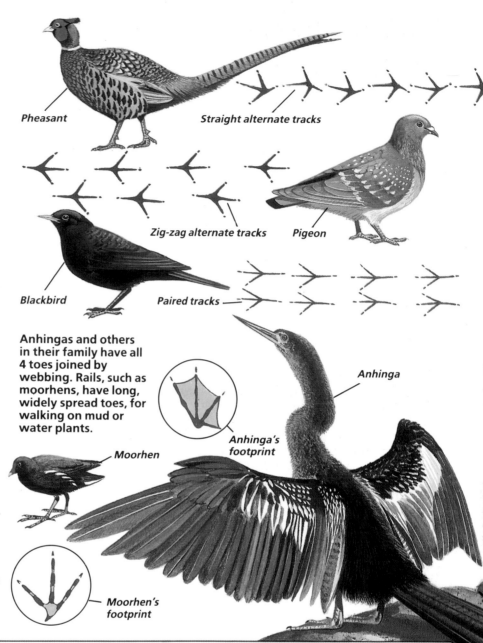

Anhinga

Anhinga's footprint

Moorhen

Moorhen's footprint

Black swan

Gulls and waterfowl have their 3 forward-facing toes connected by webbing.

Grebes and coots have lobed toes. Each toe has a separate web.

Great crested grebe

Making casts of tracks

Tracks in smooth, partly dried mud give the best plaster casts. It is not possible to take casts from snow or dry sand, but wet sand may work. You will need some plaster of Paris (modelling plaster), water in a small bowl, a strip of thin cardboard about 3x30cm (1x12in), newspaper a paper-clip and a spoon.

1. Form cardboard into a circle. Fasten with paper-clip. Place circle around print and press down gently.

Build up soil outside circle to block any gaps.

2. Stir plaster into water to make a thick, creamy mixture and pour onto print in circle. Leave for at least 15 minutes to set.

Plaster goes warm as it sets. Do not move cast until cold again.

3. Lift cast carefully and wrap in newspaper. Once home, unwrap and leave for several hours to dry and harden. Wash the cast to clean it.

Beaks

Birds' beaks (or bills) vary greatly in appearance and perform a wide range of functions including feeding, preening and nest-building. Some birds also use their beaks during courtship and in fights. Beaks are made up of two bony parts called mandibles. The upper mandible is attached to the main part of the skull (called the cranium). The lower mandible is joined to the lower jaw bone. The bony parts are covered by a light, horny sheath. The whole beak grows continuously to counteract wear and tear.

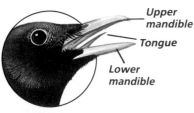

Upper mandible

Tongue

Lower mandible

A blackbird has a general-purpose shaped beak for feeding on a mixed diet of insects, worms and fruit.

Toucans, such as this keel-billed toucan, use their huge bills to reach fruit in the rainforest. The bills may also help the birds recognize one another.

Outer layer of bill is a horny sheath.

Bill has jagged edge for gripping fruit.

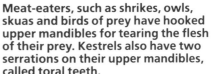

Beak shapes

Different beak shapes have evolved for eating different types of food. By looking at a bird's beak you can often get an idea of the kind of food it eats.

Insect-eaters, such as warblers, generally have thin, pointed beaks for picking insects from leaves and bark.

Wood warbler

Seed-eaters, such as finches, have strong, chunky beaks for cracking open the hard shells of seeds and nuts.

Greenfinch

Meat-eaters, such as shrikes, owls, skuas and birds of prey have hooked upper mandibles for tearing the flesh of their prey. Kestrels also have two serrations on their upper mandibles, called toral teeth.

Kestrel

Geese, swans and most ducks have flattish bills for dabbling on water surfaces for tiny animals, plants and plant seeds. They can sieve food from water and mud with their wide beaks. Some also up-end to get food from deep water.

Green-winged teal

Nectar-feeders, such as honeyeaters, have thin, pointed bills, often down-curved for reaching into long, tubular flowers.

Brush-like tongue for sucking nectar

White-plumed honey-eater

Herons, storks, grebes, cranes and terns have long, straight dagger-shaped bills for catching fish.

Grey heron

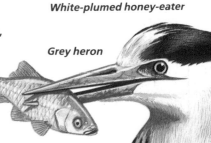

Avoiding competition

Within each group (seed-eaters, insect-eaters etc), the beaks of different species vary in shape and size and also have subtle adaptations. This prevents too many birds from competing for the same types of food. Seed-eating finches, for example, have a wide range of beak shapes.

A crossbill can split the scales of fir cones with the crossed tips of its bill, to get at seeds.

A goldfinch probes thistles and teasles for seeds with its fine, pointed bill.

A hawfinch can crack olive and cherry stones with its large, strong beak.

Waders

Waders (shorebirds) have narrow beaks, adapted for searching for food on soft mud and sandy shores. The variation, especially in beak length, that has evolved within this group allows many different species to feed in the same place without competition.

Oystercatchers use their long bills to prise or hammer open shellfish.

Avocets sweep their slender, curved bills from side to side in shallow water to filter tiny crustaceans.

Turnstones move stones with their stout bills to find small crabs and sandhoppers.

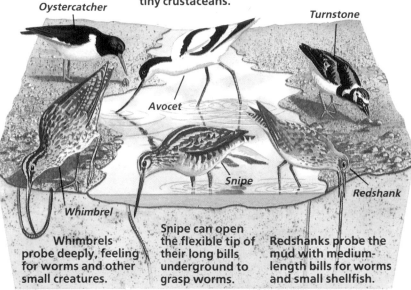

Oystercatcher

Avocet

Turnstone

Snipe

Redshank

Whimbrel

Whimbrels probe deeply, feeling for worms and other small creatures.

Snipe can open the flexible tip of their long bills underground to grasp worms.

Redshanks probe the mud with medium-length bills for worms and small shellfish.

Other uses of beaks

Some birds develop more ornate or colourful beaks for the breeding season. Puffins, for example, grow big, colourful bills which they use for attracting a mate and digging nesting burrows. The extra parts, or plates, which make a beak more ornate, are shed after breeding, leaving a smaller, duller beak.

Tufted puffins "billing" (rubbing bills together as part of courtship).

Woodpeckers, such as this pileated woodpecker, use their beaks to mark territory by drumming on trees.

Starlings, like many birds, use their beaks in fights and warning displays.

Fulmars belong to a group of birds called tubenoses. These birds have tube-shaped nostrils in their beaks from which it is thought excess salt is excreted. They also have an excellent sense of smell.

Nostrils

Songs and calls

All birds use calls to communicate with one another, but it is mainly songbirds (in the order *Passeriformes* – see page 47) that produce the more complicated, tuneful sounds, called songs. A song or call may be the only evidence of a bird's presence, and with practice, it is possible to identify birds just from the sounds they make. Many birds, especially secretive ones and nocturnal species, such as owls and nightjars, are much more often heard than seen.

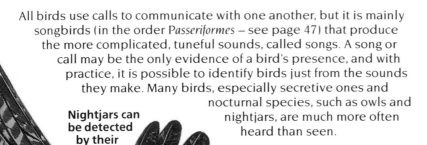

Nightjars can be detected by their purring calls.

Sonograms

To study songs and calls, ornithologists use a machine called a sound spectograph. It translates sound waves into the movements of a pen, drawing a graph called a sound spectogram or sonogram.

Sonogram of the call of a nightjar

Singing habits

In most species, only males sing. They do so mostly in the breeding season, to establish and maintain ownership of a territory and to attract a mate. A song may be repeated over a thousand times a day. The males that can sing the most variations of their species' song tend to attract mates first. Once a bird has attracted a mate, he sings less often or may stop entirely. Nightingales can sing hundreds of variations of their species' song. They sing during the day from concealed spots and also at night when most other birds are roosting. Once they have attracted a mate, they stop singing. Some birds, such as cactus wrens, defend territories all year and so keep singing all year round.

Nightingales sing at night and by day.

Cactus wrens sing all year round.

Song posts

The males of some species sing from prominent points around their territories, such as television aerials, the tops of trees, roofs, fence posts or telephone poles. A bird will regularly use the same selection of song posts. Other species, such as blackcaps and goldcrests, usually use concealed song posts.

Meadowlark on song post

Song learning

Birds are born with the ability to sing the basic song of their species, but only in a simple form. More complicated forms of the song have to be learned from parents or from other birds during the first year. Some birds can only learn their own song but other species can learn the "wrong" song. This was shown when zebra finches were reared by Bengalese finches and learned their song. They kept singing the "wrong" song even when returned to a zebra finch colony.

Colony of zebra finches

Calls

Some species have over 20 different calls, each with a distinct purpose. There are, for example, calls for keeping in contact within a group, calls for birds to recognize each other in colonies and alarm calls to warn of danger.

A gannet returning to its nest in a crowded colony with food for its mate makes a simple, squawky call. The nesting bird calls back, guiding its mate to their nest.

Learning bird sounds

Learning to recognize birds' songs and calls is not easy, but the following tips will help you.

● Begin before the nesting season when only a few birds are singing. Track these species down and get to know their songs.

● As new species come into song, try to learn their songs and calls as well. By starting with a few species, you will know when you hear something different.

● Visit a new habitat with a more experienced birdwatcher who knows the songs and calls of the birds there and can teach you.

● Listen to recordings of bird songs on tape, record or CD. You may be able to borrow them from a lending library.

Long-tailed tits live in small flocks in winter. They make dry, churring calls and high-pitched "zee"s to keep in contact as they move around.

When guillemot chicks are played tapes of their parents' calls and those of other guillemots, they only react to the former, pecking the speaker and begging for food.

Alarm calls

Alarm calls are usually short and sharp so that potential predators do not have time to locate the bird making them. A call may be a general alarm or, in the case of songbirds, may give an indication of where the predator is.

Stonechats give an alarm when a predator is far off. Other birds often rely on them for an early warning.

Mimicry

Some birds, such as starlings and jays, learn the calls and songs of other species. It is not known for certain why they do this, but in some cases it may protect them.

Jays have been known to mimic the call of a tawny owl to frighten enemies away from their chicks.

Recording bird song

You can make your own recordings of bird song using a portable tape recorder and a microphone. The microphone can be taped to a branch or post that is used as a song post.

Songpost
Microphone
Tape recorder

Cover the microphone with a thin layer of foam rubber to help reduce wind noise.

Professional recordists use a piece of equipment called a parabolic reflector to help cut out background noise. You can make your own from a cardboard cone. Tape the microphone into the cone. Experiment to find the best position for recording.

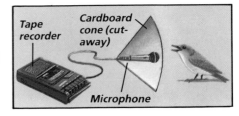

Tape recorder
Cardboard cone (cut-away)
Microphone

Senses and signals

Sight and hearing are a bird's two most important senses. They are used to find food, detect danger and in communication. As well as using sounds, birds often communicate by visual signals with body postures and displays to show intentions or feelings. Birds in open habitats are more likely to use visual signals than those in dense vegetation, where sound is more important.

Threat displays

Birds use threatening postures or movements as signals to others when defending a territory or competing for food. The point of these threat displays is to make the other bird retreat, so avoiding the necessity of fighting.

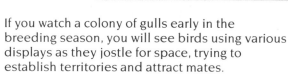

When faced by a rival, a European robin displays his breast and holds his head back.

A Philippine eagle raises the feathers on its head to form a "fright mask" in a threat display.

If you watch a colony of gulls early in the breeding season, you will see birds using various displays as they jostle for space, trying to establish territories and attract mates.

Grass-pulling – similar to pulling at an opponent's wing in a fight

Upright posture with wings held slightly out

Long call with neck stretched up

Lesser black-backed gull threat postures

Submission signals

To avoid a fight, a bird responds to aggressive behaviour by retreating or signalling submission. Submission is often shown by turning away the part of the body that is used to show aggression.

To show submission, a European jay flattens the crest on its head and points its bill upward.

Distraction displays

When protecting eggs and young, ground-nesting birds may move away from their nests and do a conspicuous display to try to distract a predator. A killdeer lures a predator away by dragging a wing and pretending she cannot fly. Once the predator is safely away from the nest, she flies off.

Distraction display of killdeer

Hearing

A bird's ears are positioned on either side of its head behind its eyes. The openings are covered by feathers which do not normally have barbules, so sound can be picked up more easily. What appear to be "ears" on some owls are tufts used in display and have nothing to do with hearing.

Ear

Scarlet macaw

In many owls, one ear is larger and often higher up than the other. The tiny difference in the time taken for sounds to reach the inner ears lets these owls pinpoint a noise and locate prey even in darkness.

Skull of Tengmalm's owl showing position of ear openings

Right ear opening

Left ear opening

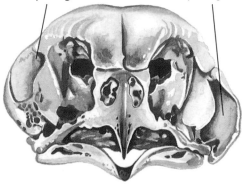

Eyes and eyesight

Birds depend more on eyesight for survival than on anything else. Their vision is sharp and powerful. In some species, such as hawks, it is ten times better than our own. In relation to their body size, birds' eyes are very large. Although they cannot move their eyeballs as much as we can, they can move their heads more to make up for this.

An eagle owl hunts at night. Its large eyes, which are the same size as our own, allow it to see well even in dim light.

Most birds' eyes are on the sides of their head which gives them a wide field of view (area they can see) for keeping a look-out. There is, however, only a small area of binocular vision where the fields of view of the two eyes overlap. Binocular vision enables animals to judge distances accurately and so pinpoint prey.

Field of view of sparrow

Area of binocular vision

Birds of prey, such as owls, have forward-facing eyes. This gives them a smaller field of view but a wider area of binocular vision for hunting. Owls cannot move their eyeballs at all, but have very flexible necks to make up for this.

Area of binocular vision

Field of view of owl

Like other owls, a barn owl has a very flexible neck.

Birds have an extra eyelid, called a nictitating membrane, which can cover the eye to protect and moisten it without loss of vision. It is used in bright sunlight, in flight and by birds that dive under water.

Nictitating membrane of a king vulture.

The eyes of some waders, such as woodcocks, are positioned in a way that allows them to see all around, even when feeding. They have binocular vision behind their heads and at the tips of their beaks.

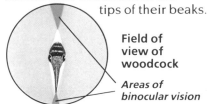

Field of view of woodcock

Areas of binocular vision

Courtship

During the breeding season you may see birds taking part in courtship activities before mating, nesting and raising their young. For some species, courtship lasts only a few minutes. For others it involves long, complicated visual and vocal displays. Many birds develop colourful breeding plumage to help them attract a mate.

In spring, a male indigo bunting has blue breeding plumage when the brown edges of his feathers have worn away.

The purpose of courtship is to bring about successful mating between birds of the same species. The initial activities often help birds to find out if they are courting a bird of the other sex and of the same species.

A male black woodpecker (right) has a larger red cap than a female. By turning away, the birds find out each other's sex.

A few species mate with many partners, but most only have one at a time. Some, such as swans, stay together for life. Each pair still performs a courtship ceremony every year before mating, though. This strengthens their relationship which is called a pair-bond.

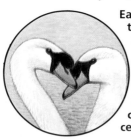

Each year, as the breeding season approaches, pairs of mute swans perform graceful courtship ceremonies.

Raggiana bird of paradise

Birds of paradise shriek, puff out their chests and show off their tail plumes in display.

Courtship displays

Courtship displays, made up of special calls and movements, are mainly performed by males who may make use of their colourful plumage. As well as trying to attract a mate, displays may send out messages, such as where a bird has found a nest-site.

When a blue-footed booby wants to attract a mate, he raises his tail and struts around, lifting his feet high in the air.

If the female shows no interest, he raises his wings, points his beak up and whistles loudly.

An interested female responds by touching the male's neck with her bill.

Lek displays

Some males gather each year to display on communal grounds called "leks". Each male "owns" a small area. Senior males have areas in the centre. The noisy, energetic displays last for hours. When females arrive, they head towards the centre to mate. There are no lasting pair-bonds.

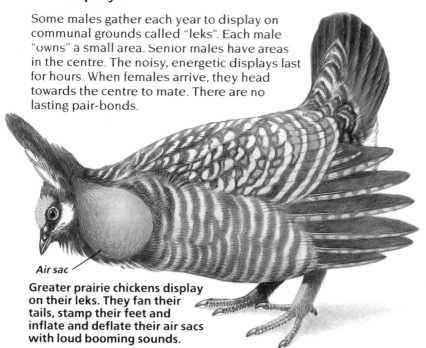

Air sac

Greater prairie chickens display on their leks. They fan their tails, stamp their feet and inflate and deflate their air sacs with loud booming sounds.

Bowerbirds

Male bowerbirds make elaborate bowers from sticks and grasses, solely to attract females. They decorate them with shells, feathers, flowers and even man-made objects, such as glass. Females visit at least three bowers before choosing a mate. When a female approaches, the male picks up one of the objects and does a display, strutting around, cackling and hissing.

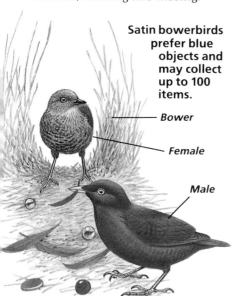

Satin bowerbirds prefer blue objects and may collect up to 100 items.

Bower

Female

Male

Mating

Courtship normally leads to mating which usually lasts less than ten seconds. During this time, the male's sperm is transferred to the female to fertilize the eggs inside her body. The male stands on the female's back and she moves her tail to one side so that her opening, called a cloaca, comes into contact with his.

A male bee-eater hovers above the female and lands on her back to mate. He flaps his wings to keep his balance.

Mutual displays

In species where male and female look similar, both may take part in a long, dance-like display on land, in the water or even in the air. This strengthens pair-bonds and brings both birds into a similar emotional state so that mating can occur. Great crested grebes perform one of the most elaborate dances.

First a single grebe swims around calling loudly to announce that it is looking for a mate.

One bird approaches the other, low in the water with wings arched.

The birds face each other and waggle their heads. This occurs several times during the display.

The pair may dive to pull up weeds then swim together and rise up to offer each other the weeds.

This display, with the body held flat, is performed near the nest site. It shows that the bird is ready to mate. Mating often takes place on a floating, raft-like nest which the birds build from weeds and sticks.

Nests

The nesting season is a particularly interesting time for ornithologists, since birds are very active and visible as they collect nesting materials and food for their young. At the start of the season they are busy finding sites where their nests will be safe from predators. Some choose well-hidden sites or ones that are hard to reach. Others rely on camouflage.

Kittiwakes, like many other seabirds, nest in colonies on inaccessible cliffs.

Northern orioles make bag-like nests suspended from twigs by plant fibres and hair. They are high above the ground at the ends of branches.

Pairs of European kingfishers rear their young inside tunnel-shaped burrows in riverbanks.

Northern oriole's nest

Urban nesting sites

Many species nest in or near buildings and there are ways you can encourage birds to nest (see pages 42-44). You must, however, resist the temptation to look at nests. Any disturbance may make the adults desert the young. You can watch for nesting signs (see opposite) and look for old nests at the end of the season.

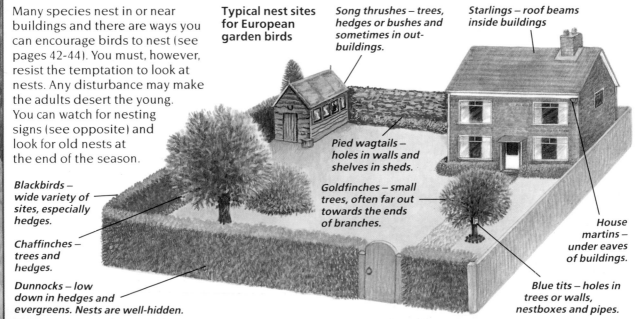

Typical nest sites for European garden birds

Song thrushes – trees, hedges or bushes and sometimes in out-buildings.

Starlings – roof beams inside buildings

Pied wagtails – holes in walls and shelves in sheds.

Goldfinches – small trees, often far out towards the ends of branches.

House martins – under eaves of buildings.

Blackbirds – wide variety of sites, especially hedges.

Chaffinches – trees and hedges.

Dunnocks – low down in hedges and evergreens. Nests are well-hidden.

Blue tits – holes in trees or walls, nestboxes and pipes.

Types of nests

Birds use a wide range of materials for making nests and each species has its own design and method of construction, so nests vary greatly in appearance, shape and size. Some hummingbirds' nests are only 2cm (1in) wide, whereas a mallee fowl's may be 4.5m (15ft) across. Many birds make cup-shaped nests. Some are lined with mud, others with feathers and hair.

Rufous fantail

Tailor birds make nests from large leaves. They sew them together with strands of cotton using their feet and beaks.

Long-tailed tailor birds

Swallows and house martins gather mud and use it to construct mud cups, which they "glue" onto ledges and walls.

House martins

Long-tailed tits make dome-shaped nests from mosses, lichens and cobwebs.

Long-tailed tit

King and emperor penguins do not make nests at all. The female lays one egg which the male keeps warm on his feet, under a flap of skin.

Male emperor penguin

Mallee mounds

Mallee fowl use the heat given off by rotting plants to keep their eggs warm inside their huge nests.

Sand

First the male scoops out a large pit. He fills it with leaves and twigs, waits for it to rain and covers them with a layer of sand.

Vegetation

As the plants rot, they heat the nest and the female lays an egg in a hole the male has dug. She lays one egg every week for 6 months.

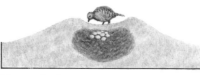

The male frequently tests the temperature with his beak and adds or removes sand to keep the nest at a constant 33°C (91°F).

Mallee fowl chick

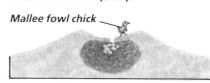

After about 60 days, a chick hatches and makes its way to the surface. It can fend for itself as soon as it leaves the nest.

A fantail's nest is shaped like a wineglass.

Nesting signs

Even though you cannot always see nests, as they are often well-hidden, there are plenty of other signs which show that birds are nesting. Here are some to look out for.

● Bird singing on a song post every day to mark territory.

● Birds visiting possible nest sites and birds carrying food for young.

● Birds carrying nesting material to nest or droppings away from nest.

Song thrush

● Birds which have just fledged (left the nest).

● Parent trying to lure predators away from nest with a distraction display (see page 27).

● Hatched egg shells on the ground – often some distance away from the nest.

Eggs and young

Eggs, like the birds that lay them, vary greatly in appearance. The clutch size (the number of eggs a bird lays) depends on the species and also on factors such as a female's age and health, the time of year, the habitat and the amount of food available. Blue tits have been known to lay 19 eggs in a clutch. Albatrosses lay only one.

It is illegal to touch or handle wild birds' eggs, but you can see old collections at natural history museums.

The colour or shape of an egg may be vital in ensuring its safety. Hole-nesting species, such as owls, often have white or pale eggs which can be seen easily in dim light so parents do not tread on them. Camouflaged eggs are common for ground-nesting species, such as lapwings and larks. Guillemot eggs vary widely in appearance. This may help parents to recognize their own eggs among thousands of eggs in a colony. Guillemot eggs are laid directly onto a bare cliff ledge. The pointed shape of the eggs means that if one is accidentally knocked, it will roll round in a circle, and not off the ledge.

If knocked, a pointed egg rolls round in a circle.

Emu egg

American robin egg

Common snipe egg

Albatross egg – the largest of any seabird

Herring gull egg

Little owl egg

Spotted flycatcher eggs

Broad billed hummingbird egg – the smallest of any species

Guillemot egg

Killdeer lay camouflaged eggs in a shallow hole scraped from the stony ground. The young are also well camouflaged.

A western grebe's clutch of three or four eggs are laid at intervals of about two or three days. An egg is pale blue when it emerges, but turns chalky white as it dries. The eggs then gradually become darker as they absorb brown stains from the damp nesting material.

Western grebe laying an egg

Raft-like nest

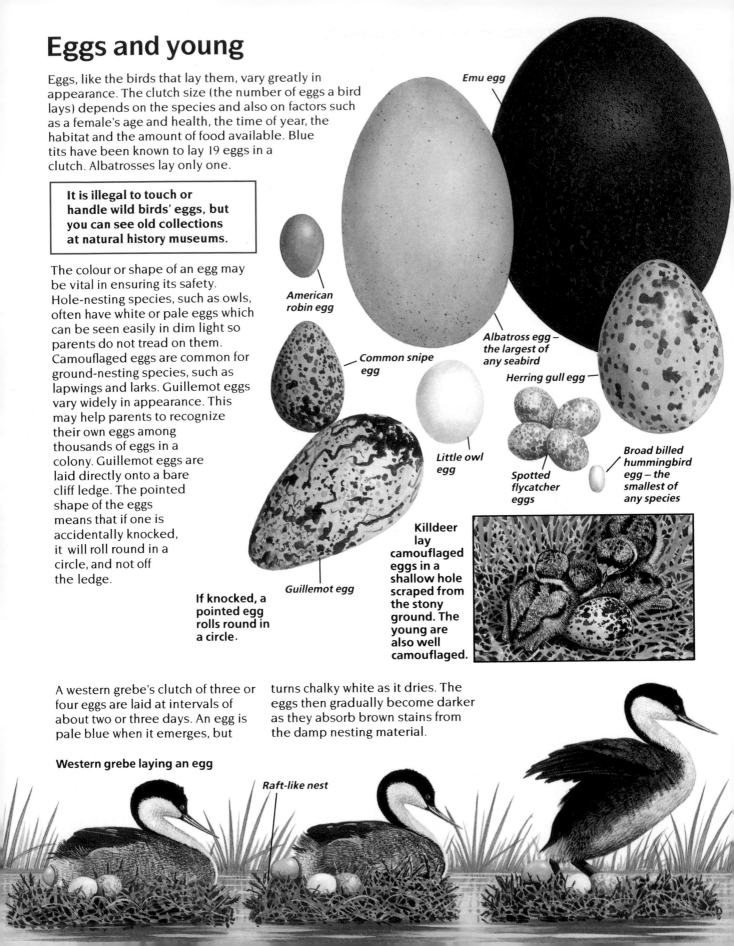

Incubation

Parents sit on their eggs to keep them at a temperature near their own blood heat. This is incubation. It lasts about two weeks for small birds, but much longer for larger ones – over 80 days for some albatrosses. Before incubation, feathers are moulted from parts of the parent's belly. These areas (called brood patches), which have blood vessels just below the skin, touch the eggs. In most species, both parents share the care of eggs and

A marsh tit has one brood patch.

young, though in some it is only the female or in a few cases, just the male. Over 70 species, including cuckoos and some cowbirds, play no part in raising young, abandoning eggs in other species' nests.

A cuckoo's egg is similar in size and shape to the host's – in this case a dunnock's.

Hatching and growing

When a bird is ready to hatch, it chips its way out of its egg. Many birds have an "egg tooth" on their beak to help them. This drops off soon after hatching. Young birds can be difficult to identify. The best way is to look at their parents, though some field guides do deal specifically with eggs and young birds. The young of most birds are blind, naked and unable to walk when they hatch. These young (described as nidicolous) are totally dependent on their parents until they gain strength, grow feathers and can leave the nest. While in the nest they are known as nestlings. When they leave they are called fledgelings. The young of other species have their eyes open and can leave the nest and feed themselves soon after hatching. These young (which are described as nidifugous) are covered in down or feathers and are usually called chicks.

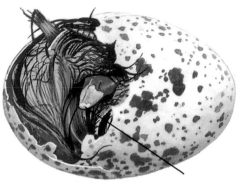

Moorhen chick hatching   *Egg tooth*

Nidifugous young, such as this three-day old lapwing chick, can leave the nest, run and feed themselves soon after hatching.

Nidicolous young, such as this three-day old blackbird nestling, stay in the nest for two weeks or more, totally dependent on their parents.

Observing nesting

Parents must work hard to find enough food for nestlings. A great tit has been known to visit its nest over 600 times a day with insects. You can find out the approximate number of visits parent birds make by watching a nest site and making records.

Blue tit visiting nestbox with food

Use binoculars to watch the birds and record the number of visits in an hour in the way shown below. This allows you to see how long it took to find food between visits.

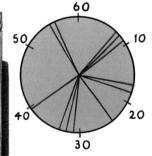

Record of blue tits visiting nestbox. Each line represents one visit.

To calculate the approximate number of times the birds visit the nest with food each day, multiply the number of visits you have recorded in an hour (in this case 12) by the number of hours of day-light at the time you are watching, for example:

12 × 17 = 204

Multiply this figure by the total number of days that the species of birds you are observing feed their young. (You should be able to find this out from a good field guide – about 19 days for blue tits), for example:

204 × 19 = 3876

Migration

Birds are the greatest travellers of the animal world. About half of all species regularly move from one habitat to another, some covering very long distances. These migrations expose birds to many dangers, such as bad weather, human hunters and predators, exhaustion and starvation. They are necessary, however, as they increase a species' chances of survival by allowing it to benefit from better food supplies or breeding conditions.

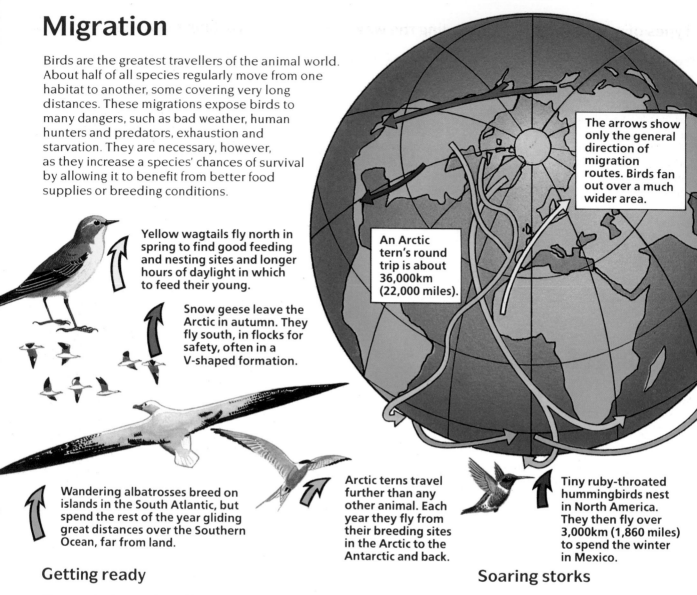

The arrows show only the general direction of migration routes. Birds fan out over a much wider area.

An Arctic tern's round trip is about 36,000km (22,000 miles).

Yellow wagtails fly north in spring to find good feeding and nesting sites and longer hours of daylight in which to feed their young.

Snow geese leave the Arctic in autumn. They fly south, in flocks for safety, often in a V-shaped formation.

Wandering albatrosses breed on islands in the South Atlantic, but spend the rest of the year gliding great distances over the Southern Ocean, far from land.

Arctic terns travel further than any other animal. Each year they fly from their breeding sites in the Arctic to the Antarctic and back.

Tiny ruby-throated hummingbirds nest in North America. They then fly over 3,000km (1,860 miles) to spend the winter in Mexico.

Getting ready

Changes in the number of hours of daylight are known to trigger migration. As the days become longer or shorter, migratory species become restless and some species begin to gather in groups.

Just before winter, martins and swallows gather on overhead wires before migrating from Europe and N.W. Asia to Africa.

Martins

Before leaving, birds build up layers of fat which are the "fuel" for their journeys. Some, such as warblers, almost double their body weight. Blackpoll warblers migrate from North to South America. They can fly non-stop for over 100 hours before having to stop to "refuel".

Warbler before and after migration. The size of the body under the feathers is shown in brown.

Before migration – weight 19g (0.8oz)

After migration – 10.5g (0.4oz)

Soaring storks

Storks and other birds which soar on outstretched wings, gain height from warm, rising air currents, called thermals. Thermals only occur over land, so storks choose routes with short sea crossings. Vast numbers use the the Straits of Gibraltar and the Bosporus when they fly from Europe to Africa.

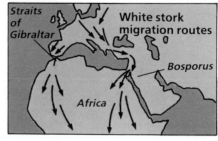

Straits of Gibraltar

White stork migration routes

Bosporus

Africa

Types of migration

The migration of some birds, such as waxwings, and nutcrackers, may follow food availability. Waxwings breed in Scandinavian and Northern European forests, feeding on berries. If berry crops fail, though, they visit other areas and may be seen as far south as Algeria. These migrations are called irruptions.

Waxwings

Some species only migrate short distances. Snow finches, mountain quails and Alpine accentors just move downhill from near the top of mountains to avoid the worst winter weather and find food. Many ducks, grebes and divers fly to the coast when their breeding lakes freeze.

Slavonian Grebes are often seen on the sea in the winter.

In many species, only part of the population migrates. Residents may be joined by migrants of the same species, mostly from further north, at certain times of the year. Resident chaffinches in southern Europe are joined by migrants from the north in winter. Others fly even further south to areas where they are found only in winter.

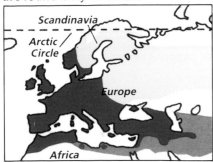

Chaffinches found only in summer
Chaffinches found all year
Chaffinches found only in winter

Finding the way

It is still not fully understood how birds find their way over long distances. It seems there are a variety of methods. Some species may use a combination of these.

Daytime migrants, such as swallows, may follow landmarks such as rivers and mountains or use the sun – they may have to stop when the sky clouds over.

Experiments with species inside planetariums (domes with artificial night skies) have shown that some can use the position of the moon and stars for navigation.

Species such as turtle doves can migrate even on cloudy nights. It is thought they can sense the earth's magnetic field and use this for navigation.

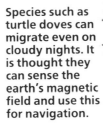

Lines of earth's magnetic field

Tracking migrants

Ornithologists use various methods to find out more about migration. The first two you can try yourself.

● Observing daytime migrants, such as cranes and storks, flying in groups – noting the direction, time and dates of flights.

● Listening for songs and calls of newly-arrived migrants, such as cuckoos in Europe in spring, and noting the date.

● Moon watching – observing the silhouettes of migrants flying across the face of the moon.

● Using radar to track the movements of large flocks.

● Using a hand-held receiver to track birds which have small radio transmitters on them (see page 40).

● Marking birds with colours, wing tags or leg bands (see page 40).

Counting birds

If you live near near a pond, lake or reservoir, you can study variations in bird numbers over a year. Count the birds once a week or once a month (see page 41 for methods) and record the data on charts. Residents may be joined by migrants for a few months.

This chart records a monthly count of coots on a lake. The residents were joined by migrants from August to March.

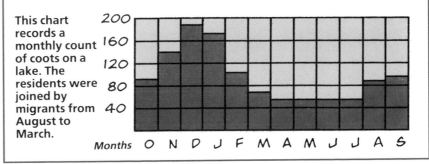

Months   O N D J F M A M J J A S

Studying a bird community

By studying an area and its birds over a period of a year or more, you can begin to build up a picture of the way bird populations and bird behaviour change from season to season. Your study will also give you practice in fieldcraft, note-taking and identification.

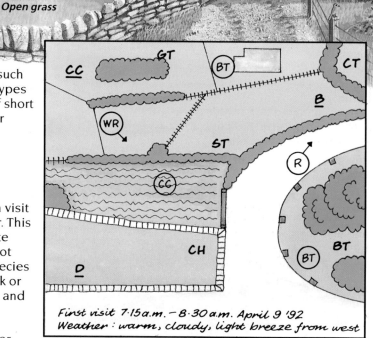

House
Conifers
Fence
Dense hawthorn
Ploughed field
Hedge
Stone wall
Open grass
Oak tree
Path

Choosing a study area

Choose an area with a variety of habitats, but not one so large that you cannot cover all of it on each visit. A suitable area could be a park, a large garden, two or three streets where you live, or the land around your school, around a church, alongside a footpath or near a lake or reservoir.

Draw a map of your area, marking major features such as roads, buildings, ponds and power lines, and types of vegetation such as hedges, large trees, areas of short grass and ploughed fields. Make several copies or photocopies of your map to use in the field.

Surveying the birds

Try to visit your study area at least once a month throughout the year. Walk the same route on each visit and make a record of all the birds you see or hear. This method of study is called a line transect. The route may weave around, but try to make sure you do not count the same bird more than once. Note the species and the number of birds you see in your notebook or on a copy of your map. You can use abbreviations and symbols as shown below the map.

Another way of surveying the birds is to visit one or more points inside your study area each time. Record all the birds that you see or hear during a short period of time (ten minutes, for example) in each place. This method of study is called a point count.

First visit 7·15 a.m. – 8·30 a.m. April 9 '92
Weather: warm, cloudy, light breeze from west

R = Robin	ST = Song thrush	CC = Chiffchaff
GT = Great tit	B = Blackbird	D = Dunnock
CT = Coal tit	CH = Chaffinch	◯ = singing
WR = Wren	BT = Blue tit	— = calling
		➜ = moving

Keeping a record

Use a notebook at all times in the field. Keep a log-book at home and transfer your information, including any sketches you make. If you have a computer, you could use it to store and analyze data. Lists and numbers of birds can be used to plot graphs, showing how numbers and species vary from month to month and season to season.

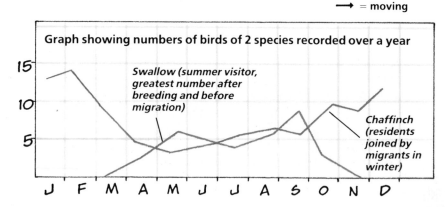

Graph showing numbers of birds of 2 species recorded over a year

Swallow (summer visitor, greatest number after breeding and before migration)

Chaffinch (residents joined by migrants in winter)

15
10
5

J F M A M J J A S O N D

Other studies

At the beginning of the breeding season, mark on copies of your map all the places where you see signs of birds nesting (see page 31), using a different map for each species. After several visits, you may be able to build up a picture of the pattern of territories for individual species and from this work out the number of breeding pairs in your study area.

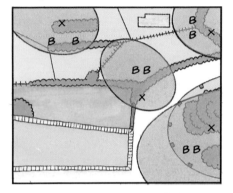

Blackbird territories marked on map. X marks probable nest sites.

Often, a bird population depends on the plants in an area for food and nest sites. Study the trees, bushes and other plants and try to answer the following questions:

● Which plants are present?

● Which birds feed from which plants and at which times of year?

● Which trees and bushes are important for nest sites? (Look for old nests in winter).

● Which trees and plants are used for song posts?

Red-winged blackbird singing in reed bed

Look out for interesting and unusual behaviour, such as threat and courtship displays, ways of feeding and food storing and anxiety of parents (showing they have young nearby). Use quick sketches as well as words to record behaviour.

Male wood duck preening female (allopreening)

Song is a clue to territories and for most species this is connected with nesting. Record the time and dates when birds are singing, especially early and late dates. Try to answer these questions:

● How early in the day do birds start to sing and how late do they continue?

● How does the weather (especially wind and temperature) affect singing?

● How much of the day is spent singing?

● When do birds find time to feed?

● Which birds sing in the air and how long (on average) do these song flights last?

● Do song flights get longer or shorter as the breeding season advances?

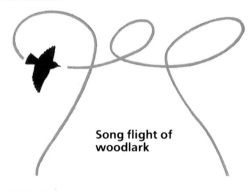

Song flight of woodlark

Going further

Local natural history societies and bird clubs collect records and they may be interested in yours, especially early and late dates of migrants, numbers of wintering wildfowl, sightings of rare birds, accurate breeding numbers and unusual behaviour.

Once you have some experience of compiling data, you could take part in official national or local surveys. These are aimed at discovering the distribution of a range of species over a country. Contact a bird organization (see page 45) to find out more.

In Britain there has been a regular national survey of grey herons since 1928 which has provided useful information about population changes, as the graph shows.

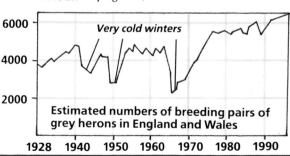

Estimated numbers of breeding pairs of grey herons in England and Wales

Very cold winters

6000
4000
2000

1928 1940 1950 1960 1970 1980 1990

Bird conservation

About one in nine of the world's bird species is in danger of extinction – at least 1,000 species. The threats to birdlife include pollution, hunting, competition from introduced species and capture for the pet trade. However, the main threat to birds and other wildlife is loss of habitat. All animals must have suitable, safe places to live, breed and rear young if they are to have any chance of survival. Some of the threats and some of the methods designed to protect birds are described on these pages.

This chart shows the percentages of birds in danger and the main threats to their survival. Some species are threatened in more than one way, so the numbers do not add up to 100.

Scarlet-breasted parrot

Over 100 parrot species (a third of the world's total) are in danger from illegal trade and habitat loss.

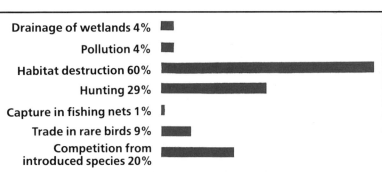

- Drainage of wetlands 4%
- Pollution 4%
- Habitat destruction 60%
- Hunting 29%
- Capture in fishing nets 1%
- Trade in rare birds 9%
- Competition from introduced species 20%

Hunting

Each year in the countries around the Mediterranean, about 900 million birds are killed as they migrate to Africa. They are shot, netted or trapped for food or sport. Much of this killing is illegal. Bird protection societies are now growing in popularity in these countries and putting pressure on governments to enforce laws and protect birds.

Honey buzzards are among birds shot in large numbers as they fly over Malta and Italy.

Habitat loss

A major cause of habitat loss is the replacement of native forests by plantations of introduced tree species. These offer few nesting or feeding opportunities for birds.

Plantation of seedling pines – unattractive to birds.

Modern farming can be disastrous for birds. The removal of hedges and trees to make larger fields and the widespread use of pesticides mean fewer safe feeding and nesting places.

Intensively farmed land attracts very few species of birds.

No habitat is richer in species than tropical rainforests, but each year an area of rainforest the size of Iceland is burned to the ground to produce farmland, and an area half this size is severely damaged by logging.

Rainforest destruction threatens many tropical birds.

Protecting habitats

One of the most successful ways to protect animals and plants is to create areas, such as national parks and reserves, which safeguard habitats for a variety of wildlife. There are already many such areas around the world, but far more are needed. Wetland reserves are especially important since hundreds of species rely on them for food.

Resplendent quetzals have a safe home in the Monteverde Cloud Forest Reserve in Costa Rica, bought by the Children's Tropical Forest Project.

A lot of work, called management, is needed to encourage and maintain bird populations on a reserve. Digging ponds and channels to maintain water levels or to create wetlands helps attract wetland species. Planting native trees and removing introduced ones creates an attractive habitat for a variety of woodland birds. Building structures such as nest platforms, nestboxes and islands in lakes, may encourage birds to nest.

Reedbeds need a lot of work to prevent them being overgrown by other plants. They are vital habitats for rare birds.

Helping on a reserve

A good way to help protect birds is to volunteer to help on a reserve. Many reserves welcome and rely on volunteers. These are some of the jobs that you may get involved in.

● Doing surveys or censuses

● Putting in sluices, digging ditches or building dams to help maintain water levels

● Building or repairing hides

● Putting up, checking or cleaning out nestboxes

● Planting trees

Special help for birds

When a species gets so rare that only a few pairs are left, special help may be needed to ensure that they breed. White-tailed sea eagles became extinct in Britain in the early 20th century from hunting. Young birds from Scandinavia have now been released back into Scotland. So far, this reintroduction has been a success.

White-tailed sea eagle

Ospreys in Britain were hunted almost to extinction. A pair from Scandinavia returned to breed in Scotland in 1954. Their nests have been guarded night and day and about 50 pairs are now established.

A tree where ospreys had nested was vandalized in 1986. The nest and tree were repaired and the ospreys returned.

Sometimes an endangered species can be moved to an area where it can survive. In New Zealand, the Conservation Department is trying to move all the kakapos to islands which have fewer of the introduced predators which have caused their decline. It can take over a month to track down each kakapo.

Kakapos are the world's largest and only flightless parrots.

Taking eggs or birds from the wild and breeding them in zoos to try to increase numbers (captive breeding) is only tried if all else fails. Captive-bred birds will not survive when reintroduced if the conditions which endangered them still exist. Eggs of Californian condors have been hatched in San Diego Zoo, USA. The first birds have now been released into a reserve.

Californian condor chicks are fed by a condor glove-puppet "mother".

Condor chick

Glove-puppet "mother"

Looking after sick birds is not part of conservation, but sometimes necessary, for instance after oil spills at sea. Oil kills birds and if they are to survive, it must be cleaned off quickly. Even so, few survive. If you find an injured bird, contact an animal welfare organization.

Cleaning oil off a penguin

Professional ornithology

Ornithology as a career involves a great number of different activities and skills. These pages describe some of them. Professional ornithologists work in bird observatories, museums and universities and for scientific and conservation organizations.

Marking birds

A lot of what we now know about birds and their lives is a result of marking them. Birds of the same species usually look alike, and many birds travel long distances or hide in vegetation, so finding out about their movements and behaviour can be difficult. Small, coded rings* attached to birds' legs allow ornithologists to recognize individual birds if they are recaptured or found dead, and so work out their migration patterns and life spans.

Lightweight rings for different types of birds (shown life-size)

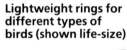

Trained ringers apply rings with special pliers. This does not hurt the birds.

Leg rings may be difficult to see from a distance, so for some species, such as large birds of prey, wing tags may be used.

Wing tag on buzzard

A radio transmitter attached to a bird allows its movements to be tracked. This is used especially on nocturnal birds, ones which live in dense vegetation and on birds of prey.

For tracing a particular group of birds (especially pale coloured ones), ornithologists may mark parts of birds with a harmless dye. The marked birds can then be recognized from a distance.

Knots with orange bellies. Other birds do not seem to react to the unusual colour.

*US = bands

Catching birds

Various methods are used to catch birds for marking. Fine nets, known as mist nets, are often used. These hold birds firmly but safely until they can be released by a ringer.

Mist nets on mudflats

For larger birds, a method called cannon-netting may be used. Rolled nets, with weighted edges, are set around feeding or roosting areas. The nets are fired over the birds using cannons or rockets.

Cannon-netting Canada geese

The Heligoland trap is a large funnel of wire-netting that leads to a corridor with a catching box at the end. Birds that land in front of the tunnel are carefully driven towards the box.

Heligoland trap

Catching box

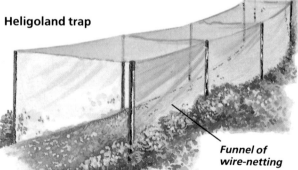

Funnel of wire-netting

When a bird is caught for marking, it is also weighed and measured before release. Its weight may show how far it will migrate, since birds store up large amounts of fat before migration (see page 34).

Finding marked birds

If you find a marked bird, send the details of the code on the ring or tag, where and when the bird was found and whether it was alive or dead, to a national ornithological organization. They may later tell you where the bird was marked and how far it had travelled. Do not remove a ring from a live bird. Small birds are very fragile. Hold them gently, as shown here, to look at details on the ring.

Holding a wheatear to look at the ring on its leg

Bird observatories

Bird observatories are places for the scientific study of birds. They are usually by the coast, often in a remote area. The ornithologists who work there monitor local bird populations and record movements and migration. Many observatories welcome experienced birdwatchers and amateur ornithologists who want take part in the studies. Contact one of the organizations listed on page 45 if you want to find out more.

Expeditions

Many species of birds live in, or migrate to, parts of the world such as remote islands, Arctic tundra, deserts, oceans, tropical forests and Antarctica. Scientific expeditions are needed to find out more about the wildlife of these areas. An expedition usually has a particular aim, such as to find out about the habitat of an endangered species and to monitor its numbers.

An expedition may include photographers who record details of the birds.

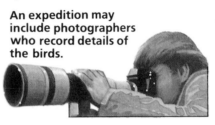

Sea watching

Sea birds, such as shearwaters, sea ducks and petrels, are especially difficult to study. The best method is "sea watching" from a headland or off-shore island. The aim is to scan the sea as far as the horizon and record any birds on or over the sea. Notes are made of all species seen over a period of time (half an hour, for example) with details of the number of birds and the direction they are going.

Sea watching is best done by 2 people – one observes and the other takes notes of directions and species. A telescope is useful and binoculars are essential.

Estimating flock sizes

Being able to estimate the size of a flock is an essential skill, especially for recording migrating birds. You cannot count every bird in a large flock as they fly past, so count part of the flock quickly, and then estimate what proportion this is of the whole. For example, if you count 10 birds and estimate that this is a tenth of the total, the whole flock is about 100 birds.

Start by working out the size of flocks on the ground or in pictures, then count each bird to check your accuracy.

Going further

If you are thinking about turning an interest in birds into a career, these are some guidelines which may help you. Remember, however, that there are many opportunities to carry out studies as an amateur. You do not need special training to enjoy watching and studying birds.

● Try out your birdwatching skills whenever and wherever possible. There is no substitute for hours spent in the field observing birds.

● Get involved with ornithological organizations in your free time.

● Help with ornithological surveys, censuses and counts.

● Visit a local bird-ringing group. If this aspect of ornithology interests you, find out how to train for a ringing licence.

● Specialize in science subjects at school, especially biology, if you have a choice.

● If you go on to higher education, choose one or more Natural Science subjects, such as zoology, ecology, environmental science or biology.

Bird projects

On the following four pages are some ideas for things that you can do to help you observe birds and to provide them with safe nesting or feeding places. Some of the projects are simple, but others are more complex and need specialized equipment and help from an adult.

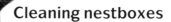
Song thrush

Nestboxes

Put up nestboxes in the winter, so that they are in position in good time for the nesting season. Boxes can be bought from pet shops and garden centres, or you could make your own (see page 44). First watch the species which visit the area where you want to put up the nestbox. The box's entrance hole must be of a suitable size for these birds.

A 27mm (1⅛in) hole suits birds the size of blue tits, coal tits, chickadees and thornbills.

Bluebirds will nest in a box with a hole measuring 38mm (1½in).

Species such as pied wagtails, European robins and flycatchers prefer an open-fronted box.

Use nails to fix the box to a tree or post, in a place where the sun will not shine directly into the hole, but not hidden by dense leaves. Put it at a height of 3-5m (6-10ft), out of the reach of cats. Many birds are fiercely territorial with their own species, so do not put boxes with the same size hole near each other.

Cleaning nestboxes

Nesting material contains insect eggs, larvae and fleas which can infect nestlings. Clean out boxes before winter, when they may be used for roosting. Use detergent and water, not insecticide.

Feeding times

The best time to feed birds is in winter when natural food supplies are low. Cheese, fat, nuts, dried fruit and baked potatoes (chopped in half) are all ideal for providing a high-energy diet. You can also buy wild birdseed from pet shops. Peanuts are very popular, but do not put out salted or dry-roasted peanuts. Do not provide food during the breeding season, as nestlings need natural food, such as insects and grubs.

Nuthatch

If you have a bird table, experiment to find the place which encourages most species and where birds can be seen easily.

Birds need water for drinking and bathing. An old refuse bin lid on bricks makes a simple bird bath. Remember to break the ice in cold weather.

Wedge lumps of fat or cheese into bark for tits and nuthatches.

Nutfeeder

Blue tit

Starlings

Song thrush

Scatter food on the ground for species such as blackbirds and song thrushes.

Blackbird

A milk carton bird-feeder

To make a simple bird-feeder, you will need two clean, empty milk cartons, a pencil, sharp scissors, a stapler and some garden wire.

1. Use the stapler to close up the top of one carton, draw and cut along the lines shown in the picture.

Cut carefully along the lines.

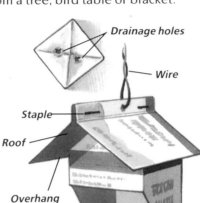

Staples

9cm (3 ½in)

3.5cm (1 ½in)

2. Cut two sides from the other carton, leaving them joined. Use scissors to score a line 1cm (⅓in) each side of the join. Fold along these lines to form the roof.

Fold the sides outwards along the lines.

Scored line

Folded join

3. Make two drainage holes in the base and staple on the roof, making sure that it overhangs the hole. Push a pencil through the feeder to make a perch. Nail the feeder to a post or tree or use wire to hang it from a tree, bird table or bracket.

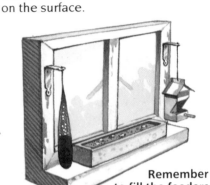

Drainage holes

Wire

Staple

Roof

Overhang

Pencil

Feeding stations

If you do not have a garden, set up a feeding station on a sheltered window sill. Get permission to attach brackets to the window frame and hang feeders from them. You could use a window-box as a feeding area. Fill it almost to the top with soil and put the food on the surface.

Remember to fill the feeders regularly in winter.

European robin

Greenfinch

Great tit

Plants for birds

Plants which provide shelter, safe nesting places and food will help attract birds to a garden.

Berry-producing shrubs, such as bereberis, rowan, holly, hawthorn and cotoneaster provide food and nest sites for many birds.

Thrush on hawthorn

Ivy provides a nest site for many birds. Its berries provide food in winter.

Blackbird on ivy

The seed heads of teasles, thistles, and sunflowers may attract finches. Sunflower seeds can also be put on bird tables.

Female bullfinch on sunflower

Making a wooden nestbox

It is possible to make your own wooden nestbox, but it is quite tricky, so ask an adult for some help. To build an open-fronted nestbox you will need a 150cm x 15cm x 2cm (60in x 6in x ¾in) plank of soft wood*, a vice or a woodworking bench, a saw, a hammer, a drill (or brace and bit), 35 40mm (1in) nails, a 15cm x 7cm (6in x 3in) strip of plastic cut from an empty cleaning liquid bottle and 8 tacks.

1. Mark lines on your wood as shown in the diagram on the left. If the width or thickness of your wood varies from those given, make sure the length of the base measures the width + the thickness of the wood. Carefully, use a saw to cut each piece. Make sure the wood is held firmly as you saw. Use sandpaper or glass-paper to smooth off any rough edges.

Roof 20cm (8in)

Side 20cm (8in) 25cm (10in)

Side 20cm (8in) 25cm (10in)

Backboard 45cm (17¾in)

Base 17cm (6½in)

Front 10cm (4in)

Extra wood

Backboard

Roof

Sides

Front

Base

This is how the pieces will fit together.

2. Carefully drill three small holes for drainage in the piece which will be the base of the box.

Drainage holes

Base

3. Assemble the box, using the hammer and nails. First join the base to the sides of the box, then nail on the front.

The "overhang" should be at the front of the box, over the shorter edges.

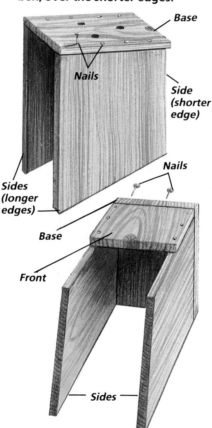

Base

Nails

Side (shorter edge)

Sides (longer edges)

Base

Nails

Front

Sides

4. Drill two holes 2.5cm (1in) from each end of the backboard, for nailing the box to a tree or post.

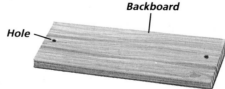

Backboard

Hole

5. Nail the backboard onto the sides and base, then nail the roof on the nestbox.

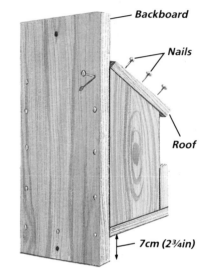

Backboard

Nails

Roof

7cm (2¾in)

6. Tack the plastic across the join.

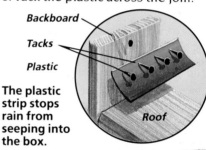

Backboard

Tacks

Plastic

Roof

The plastic strip stops rain from seeping into the box.

The finished box could be painted with a wood preservative.

* If you cannot buy a plank of these exact measurements, try to find the closest possible.

Making a bird table

To make a hanging bird table, you will need a 40cm x 30cm x 1.5cm (15in x 12in x ½in) piece of plywood, a 120cm (4ft) strip of 2.5cm x 1.5cm (1in x ½in) wood, 16 2.5cm (1in) nails, 4 screw eyes and a 2m (6ft 6in) length of garden wire.

1. Cut the strip of wood into four pieces, two measuring 35cm (13½in) and two measuring 25cm (10in).

35cm (13½in)

25cm (10in)

2. Nail the pieces along the edge of the board. Leave gaps at the corners to allow rain to drain off.

These strips stop food from blowing or rolling off.

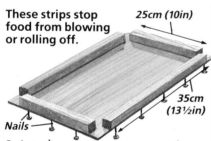

25cm (10in)

35cm (13½in)

Nails

3. Attach a screw eye near each corner (see below). Cut the wire in half and attach one piece to one of the eyes, wind it around a branch and fix it to the eye at the opposite corner. Do the same with the other piece of wire at the other side.

Hang the table in the open, at least 150cm (5ft) above the ground. Clean and clear it regularly.

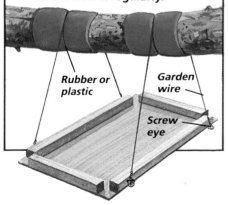

Rubber or plastic

Garden wire

Screw eye

Making a bird cake

Instead of buying ready-prepared food, you could make a bird cake using a mixture of seeds, nuts, stale cake crumbs, oatmeal or porridge oats and dried fruit. Put 500g (1lb) of the mixture into a heat-resistant bowl. Melt 250g (½lb) of solid fat in a saucepan at a low heat. Carefully pour the fat over the mixture, then leave it to set.

Useful addresses

Below are some addresses of societies and organizations which are concerned with birds and ornithology. Some of them organize clubs and activities, such as bird counts, conservation work and birdwatching trips for young ornithologists. To find out if there is a club in your area, contact one of the addresses below (remember to send a self-addressed, stamped envelope). Alternatively, your local library may be able to help.

UK

Young Ornithologists' Club (YOC), Royal Society for the Protection of Birds, The Lodge, Sandy, Bedfordshire, SG19 2DL

The YOC organizes a wide variety of activties, such as conservation work and bird-watching holidays for young people under 16. Members get a magazine and free entry into over 100 RSPB reserves in the UK.

British Trust for Ornithology, The Nunnery, Nunnery Place, Thetford, Norfolk, IP24 2PU

A scientific organization which studies birds in the environment. Activities include bird counts.

International Council for Bird Preservation, 32 Cambridge Road, Girton, Cambridgeshire, CB3 OPJ

An organization concerned with bird conservation world-wide. Their World Bird Club raises money to buy reserves and monitor the status of rare and endangered species.

Turn the cake out when it is completely cold. Do not cut it up, but put it on the bird table or feeding station whole.

The Wildfowl and Wetlands Trust, Slimbridge, Gloucestershire, GL2 7BT

The Trust is especially concerned with conservation of the world's wildfowl and wetland habitats. Activities include guided walks.

USA

National Audubon Society, 950 Third Avenue, New York, N.Y. 10022

The Audubon Society has special membership for school children called Audubon Adventures.

Canada

Canada Nature Federation/ Fédération Canadienne de la Nature, 453 Sussex Drive, Ottawa, Ontario, KIN 6Z4

The Federation can supply addresses of Natural History Societies or Bird Societies in your province.

Australia

Bird Observers Club of Australia, PO Box 185, Nunawading, Victoria, 3131

There is no separate organization for young ornithologists but you can join as a junior member.

New Zealand

Royal Forest and Bird Protection Society of New Zealand, PO Box 631, Wellington.

The Society runs the Kiwi Conservation Club for birdwatchers up to 12 years old. After that you can become a junior member of the Society. Activities include bird walks and development of reserves.

Glossary

Adult. A fully grown bird that has full **plumage** and can breed.

Alula. The four small stiff feathers on a bird's wing that help control flight.

Banding. See **Ringing**.

Bar. A natural mark across a feather or group of feathers.

Belly. The underpart of a bird between its **breast** and tail.

Binocular vision. Vision where the **fields of view** of two eyes overlap. Binocular vision enables ▶ birds to judge distances.

Breast. The part of a bird's body between its throat and **belly**.

Breeding season. The time of year when birds build nests, mate, lay eggs and raise young.

Brood. The young from a single **clutch** of eggs.

Brooding. Sitting on young to keep them warm.

◀ **Brood patch.** A small area on the **belly** from which feathers have been shed and under which eggs are kept warm.

Chick. The usual name for young birds which have their ▶ eyes open and can run soon after hatching.

Clutch. The eggs of a bird in its nest.

Colony. A group of birds of the same species nesting together.

Contour feathers. The small, overlapping feathers on the body of bird which protect it and help to keep it warm.

Coverts. The groups of small feathers that cover the bases of flight and tail feathers.

Crown. The top of a bird's head.

Display. A pattern of movement used for communication, especially ▶ during courtship and in threat.

Down feathers. The small feathers that form a fluffy layer under the **contour feathers** of an **adult** and help to keep it warm, or the first fluffy covering of a baby bird.

Eclipse plumage. The dull **plumage** of male ducks and other species after the **breeding season**.

Egg tooth. A tiny lump on the upper **mandible** of many baby birds which helps them chip through the egg shell.

Fieldcraft. The techniques and skills that are needed to get close to birds in the field without disturbing them.

Field guide. A book of bird ▶ identification.

Field mark. A natural mark on a bird, such as a wing **bar**, that can help you to identify a species.

Field of view. The area that is seen through a ▶ pair of binoculars or the area that a bird can see.

Flank. The area on the side of a bird's body.

Fledgeling (also spelled **fledgling**). A young bird that has grown its first set of feathers and has left the nest.

Flock. A group of birds of the same species feeding or travelling together.

Immature plumage (also called **sub-adult plumage**). The set of feathers which a bird has after **moulting** its **juvenile plumage**, but before it has full **adult** plumage.

Incubation. Sitting on eggs to keep them warm.

Juvenile plumage. The set of feathers in which a young bird leaves the nest.

Keel. A large extension of the breastbone to which the flight muscles are attached. ▼

Lek. An area where males of some species gather to display to females in the **breeding season**.

Mandible. One of the two parts of a bird's beak. The **upper mandible** is the top part, the **lower mandible** the bottom part.

Moulting. The process of shedding and replacing feathers.

Nape. The back of a bird's neck.

Nestling. A baby bird that is still in the nest and cannot fly.

Nictitating membrane. The extra, transparent eyelid which protects a bird's eye in flight, under water or in bright light.

◀ **Pellet.** A compact parcel of undigested food, regurgitated by some species of birds.

Plumage. A bird's feathers.

Preening. A bird's method of cleaning and looking after its feathers by drawing each one through its beak.

Primary. One of the large outer wing feathers.

Ringing (US = **banding**). Marking birds by ▶ putting small rings on their legs.

Roost. To sleep, or a place where birds sleep.

Rump. The area of a bird's body above its tail.

Secondary. One of the inner wing feathers. ▶

Shorebird. See **Wader**.

Sub-adult plumage. See **Immature plumage**.

Territory. An area occupied by a bird or group of birds.

Wader (US = **shorebird**). One of a group of birds that live close to water and use their long legs for wading in search of food.

Wetlands. Swamps, marshes and other wet areas of land.

Wildfowl. Ducks, geese and swans.

The orders of birds

This page lists the scientific names of the 23 orders of birds (see page 7) and the common family names of birds in each order

Struthioniformes
Ostrich, rheas, cassowaries, emu, kiwis.

Tinamiformes
 Tinamous.

Craciformes
Guans, chachalacas, megapodes.

Galliformes
Grouse, turkeys, pheasants, partridges, guineafowl, New World quails.

Anseriformes
Screamers, geese, swans, ducks.

Turniciformes
Buttonquails.

Piciformes
Honeyguides, woodpeckers, ▶ barbets, toucans.

Galbuliformes
Jacamars, puffbirds.

Bucerotiformes
Hornbills, ground hornbills.

Upupiformes
◀ Hoopoes, woodhoopoes, scimitarbills.

Trogoniformes
Trogons.

Coraciiformes
Rollers, ground-rollers, Courol, motmots, todies, kingfishers, bee-eaters.

Coliiformes
Mousebirds.

Cuculiformes
Cuckoos, coucals, hoatzin, roadrunners, ▶ ground-cuckoos.

Psittaciformes
Parrots.

Apodiformes
Swifts, crested ▶ swifts.

Trochiliformes
Hermits, hummingbirds.

Musophagiformes
Turacos, plantain-eaters.

Strigiformes
Owls, nightjars, frogmouths, oilbirds, potoos, nighthawks.

Columbiformes
Dodos and solitaires (extinct), pigeons ▶ and doves.

Gruiformes
Sunbittern, coots, ◀ cranes, bustards, limpkin, sungrebes, trumpeters, kagu, seriemas, rails, gallinules, mesites.

Ciconiiformes
Sandgrouse, seedsnipes, plains-wanderer, woodcocks, snipes, sandpipers, curlews, phalaropes, painted snipes, jacanas, thick-knees, sheathbills, oystercatchers, avocets, stilts, ▶ plovers, lapwings, coursers, skuas, pratincoles, skimmers, gulls, ▼

terns, auks, osprey, hawks, eagles, ▼

secretary bird, caracaras, falcons, grebes, tropicbirds, boobies, anhingas, gannets, cormorants, herons, bitterns, ▼

egrets, hammerkop, flamingos, ibises, spoonbills, shoebills, storks, pelicans, vultures, frigatebirds, divers, penguins, ▶ petrels, shearwaters, albatrosses.

Passeriformes
New Zealand wrens, pittas, broadbills, asities, Mionectine flycatchers, tyrant flycatchers, tityras, becards, cotingas, manakins, antbirds, ovenbirds, woodcreepers, ground antbirds, gnateaters, tapaculos, Australo-Papuan treecreepers, lyrebirds, scrub-birds, bowerbirds, fairywrens, emuwrens, grasswrens, honeyeaters, pardalotes, bristlebirds, scrubwrens, thornbills, Australo-Papuan robins, fairy-bluebirds, leafbirds, logrunner, chowchilla, Australo-Papuan babblers, shrikes, vireos, peppershrikes, quail-thrushes, whipbirds, Australian chough, Apostle bird, sitellas, shrike-tits, whistlers, shrike-thrushes, crows, birds-of-paradise, currawongs, wood-swallows, orioles, cuckooshrikes, fantails, drongos, monarchs, magpie-larks, ioras, bush-shrikes, helmet-shrikes, wattlebirds, rock-jumpers, rockfowls, palmchat, silky-flycatchers, waxwings, dippers, thrushes, Old World flycatchers, chats, starlings, mynas, mockingbirds, thrashers, catbirds, nuthatches, wallcreeper, treecreepers, spotted creeper, wrens, gnatcatchers, gnatwrens, tits, penduline-tits, long-tailed tits, bushtits, river-martins, swallows, kinglets, bulbuls, grey hypocolius, African warblers, white-eyes, leaf-warblers, grass-warblers, wrentit, scrub-warblers, larks, sugarbirds, flower-peckers, sunbirds, spiderhunters, berrypeckers, longbills, tit berrypecker, crested berrypecker, sparrows, rock-sparrows, pipits, accentors, weavers, estrildine finches, whydahs, olive warbler, chaffinches, Cardueline finches, Hawaiian honeycreepers, buntings, wagtails, ▶ longspurs, towhees, New World wood-warblers, tanagers, Neotropical honeycreepers, seedeaters, flower-piercers, cardinals, troupials, meadowlarks, New World blackbirds.

Bird index